To: Jermy

with love!

Sawyer Bennett

CODE NAME:
GENESIS

By
SAWYER BENNETT

ISBN: 978-1-947212-52-7

Find Sawyer on the web!
sawyerbennett.com
www.twitter.com/bennettbooks
www.facebook.com/bennettbooks

Contents

CHAPTER 1

Kynan

I NORMALLY WOULDN'T answer my phone while a gorgeous redhead was performing a strip tease in my bedroom, but it's Rachel Hart-Wright calling. As my second in charge at Jameson Force Security, she wouldn't call unless it was important. Besides, I'm just cocky enough to take a business call while receiving personal pleasure.

"This better be good, Hart," I say curtly after connecting. My gaze drifts ever so briefly to the almost-empty glass of scotch in my hand before going to the woman dry humping my bedpost to some rock song I don't recognize. She watches me through heavy-lidded eyes, knowing I'll reward her.

"I don't know if *good* is the word," she drawls. "There's a lot of money involved, but you're not going to like who it's from."

"If it's that bloody congressman who hired us to babysit his duffer son, the answer is no." That job had taught me there are some things money can't buy.

1

"What the hell is a 'duffer'?" Rachel asks.

"Someone who's useless," I say distractedly as the woman in front of me peels off her bra, exposing gloriously perky tits.

"You Brits have a funny way of talking," Rachel replies. "Why couldn't you just have said 'useless'?"

I feel the corners of my mouth turn upward into an amused smile, but she'll never know. My tone is one of impatience when I mutter, "Just tell me what the job is, and I'll approve or deny it."

"It's Joslyn Meyers."

My blood pressure instantly spikes, and I tighten my fingers so hard on my glass I'm surprised it doesn't shatter. It's difficult not to yell into the phone, but there's no mistaking the force of my words. "Not only no, but hell no. Whatever she needs, the answer is a bloody fucking no."

"I think you should listen—"

"I said 'no'," I bark into the phone but then immediately lower my voice. "Now is there anything else we need to discuss that doesn't have to do with Joslyn Meyers, or can I get back to what I was doing before you tried to ruin my night?"

"She's in serious trouble," Rachel snaps.

"Don't care," I snarl.

"Her life is in danger."

Every muscle in my body goes rigid. A slight sweat

breaks out on my forehead that has nothing to do with the redhead shimmying out of her panties. I give a hard shake of my head, wondering why Joslyn still has the power to affect me after all these years. Still, I manage to grit out between my teeth, "Don't. Care."

"That's what you want me to tell her?" Rachel asks calmly.

"I don't give a shit what you tell her, as long as the word 'no' is somewhere in your sentence." I push away every bit of the concern for Joslyn that's starting to rear its ugly head. "Refer her over to Miller's agency. They do protection detail just fine."

There's a long moment of silence as Rachel digests what I'm saying. She's well aware of my enmity toward the world-famous Joslyn Meyers, and I can't understand why she wants to fight me on this. I let my eyes roam all over the now fully naked woman—who is indeed a natural redhead—hoping it will distract me from this distasteful conversation.

"Fine," Rachel says with a sigh.

I feel elated to have this matter resolved, but I choose to ignore the fact I'm also strangely unsettled because it isn't—not for Joslyn anyway.

"I understand and respect your decision. But you can tell her yourself."

It doesn't quite penetrate what happens next because before I know it, Joslyn's soft voice comes over the line.

"Kynan," she says hesitantly.

I bolt upward in my chair, my spine stiff and unrelenting. Setting my glass on the table beside me, I see nothing even though I'm staring at the dancing woman who is now touching herself in the naughtiest way.

"Kynan," Joslyn says again. Her voice quavers with emotion. "I could really use your help."

Fuck.

I scrub a hand over my face, blinking stupidly at the woman across my bedroom as her hand works between her legs. She moans softly, but it doesn't touch me at all.

My jaw locks hard for a moment, and I tell myself to stay strong. "We're not taking on celebrity detail anymore. We can refer you to a good agency to fit your needs."

Not the full truth, but she doesn't need to know that.

The Jameson Group has expanded greatly over the last two years since I bought it from Jerico Jameson in a seven-million-dollar deal. The first thing I did was change the name to Jameson Force Security to better reflect my new business model. While the biggest chunk of our business is mainstream work—protecting celebrities and installing top-of-the-line security systems—our most lucrative contracts still came from the United States government and other foreign allies for "specialized" work that can be hard to come by.

Or more accurately... hard to get approval for. Jameson Force Security has become the go-to private security contractor. We offer the type of "off-the-books invisibility" a government might need when doing top-secret covert work.

And because the mainstream part of the business is running like a well-oiled, money-making machine and I've been getting a bit bored, I've decided to expand the covert-operations part. Because of that, Jameson Force Security was born, developed, and is now ready to take on more work.

So ready, in fact, I'm on the verge of opening a new set of offices in Pittsburgh as I need to be in better proximity to Washington, D.C. Rachel had asked me why I didn't just move to D.C., but I can't stand the place. I've always loved Pittsburgh, though. It's a city rooted in steel, grit, and determination, which is exactly the way I'd describe Jameson Force Security. I'm going to relocate to Pittsburgh and Rachel is going to stay in Vegas to run the private-security portion of the business.

"If it's a matter of money—" Joslyn says, interrupting my straying thoughts.

I cut her off. "It's not."

"Please, Kynan," she implores, and I can hear the watery tears in her voice.

Thankfully, I'm momentarily distracted when the redhead crawls on her hands and knees toward me. Blue eyes flashing with heat, her tits swaying provocatively. Silently, and with a little bit of satisfaction, I realize this woman before me is exactly what I want and need, while the woman on the phone, probably sitting in her multimillion-dollar Malibu mansion, is not.

Hands come to my thighs, slide up, and work at my belt. My cock finally deciding to get into the game, it starts to thicken at the prospect. I settle into the chair, lifting my hips briefly so she can reach inside my pants to pull me free.

I suppress a groan as her hand circles me tight and starts to stroke. Reaching out, I cup her breast, relishing the weight of it before giving her nipple a pinch. Her lush lips peel into a wicked smile right before she puts her mouth on me.

Fuck yeah. That's exactly what I need.

My hand goes to her hair, fingers gripping her fiery locks tightly. Using my grasp as a piston, I help her bob up and down, starting to get lost in the sensation.

"He almost killed me last night," Joslyn says and for a moment, her words don't register.

But then they do, and I roughly yank the redhead off my cock. Her eyes widen in surprise, but I shake my head as I sit upright in my chair again.

"What?" I manage to rasp out.

"A stalker," she whispers. "He's been harassing me for a really long time. Last night, though, he actually managed to break into my house. I couldn't get to my panic room in time."

The air in my lungs freezes. She has a panic room. Which means she's been battling a serious threat. Everything around me seems to slow as my ears ring with her revelation.

"He heard the sirens approaching before he could..." When she abruptly stops, bile rises in my throat. She coughs before finishing softly. "He ran off, and they didn't catch him."

I clear my throat from the thick emotion that has built up. "Where are you? Is someone with you now?"

Joslyn mirthlessly laughs. "I'm in your office. Over on Clarke Avenue."

She's here?

In Vegas?

"Put Rachel on the phone," I instruct, my words clipped and impersonal.

There's an indistinct murmuring between the women as the phone gets passed. Rachel's brisk and professional voice comes through. "What do you want me to do?"

Longingly, I stare at the redhead who has since moved over to lounge in a sexy pose on my bed. I want to get lost in her. Want to forget everything else.

There's no holding back the sigh of resignation that escapes me. "We're taking the case. Starting now. Bring her to my house."

"Your house?" Rachel asks in surprise.

"For safety's sake, she stays with me until I can figure out who to assign this case to."

Rachel is silent for a moment, but then murmurs, "But you're not alone."

"True," I reply as I stand. My pants barely cling to the edges of my hips. I've even lost my hard-on, a matter that needs to be rectified immediately. After I walk around the bed, I run hot eyes over the beautiful, luscious creature stretched out there. "But that's none of Joslyn's concern. We're nothing to each other but business."

"Gotcha, boss," Rachel says, clearly amused. She's known me for years. Hell, we were fuck buddies for a time. She caught me on the tail end of mine and Joslyn's breakup, and I got lost between her legs as we traveled the world in search of adventures and thrills. She was easy to talk to, so she knows the basics of what happened between us.

But Rachel and I aren't like that anymore. We've been colleagues at Jameson for over a decade. Once we started working together, it became purely professional. Since Jerico sold out to me, Rachel is the most trustworthy peer to me in this business. She's also nonjudgmental. If my treatment of Joslyn is less than civilized, Rachel won't hold it against me.

The redhead rises to her knees, then scoots toward

me. Her fingers work at the buttons of my shirt. Once it's bared, she leans in to place a kiss on the center of my chest.

My cock stirs, springing back to life, and I disconnect the call.

Joslyn is forgotten.

For the time being.

CHAPTER 2

Joslyn

"KYNAN'S DONE WELL for himself," I murmur to Rachel as we pull into the driveway of a monstrous colonial-style Spanish mansion. It's bigger than my house, which says a lot as mine sits at just over seven-thousand square feet of useless-to-me space.

"That he has," she replies as she puts her Maserati Quattroporte in park and cuts the engine.

I don't make any move to open the door. Neither does Rachel. My heart is pounding at the prospect of seeing Kynan again after all these years, but this isn't as scary as what happened last night. Unconsciously, I bring my fingers to my throat and skim over the purple bruises there.

"How old is your kid?" I ask, turning slightly toward her. She blinks in surprise, but I throw a thumb over my shoulder to the car seat in the back.

"He'll be six months on the twenty-third."

I do a quick calculation in my head before smiling. "He was almost a Christmas baby then."

"Yup." She laughs. "Bodie, my husband, insisted we make Kris his middle name in honor of the holidays."

Kris Kringle. Cute. "What's his first name?"

"Anthony, but we call him Tony."

Traditional. "Family name?"

She shakes her head with a laugh. "No. We named him after Tony Stark."

"You're kidding me?"

"I never kid about the Avengers," she says in all seriousness. Tilting her head, she considers me a moment, her smile reassuring. But my pulse spikes again when she says, "Ready to get this over with?"

I nod, but what I really want is for her to start the car again, then take me to the nearest airport and put me on a flight to somewhere no one will be able to find me. That way, I could melt into obscurity and leave the psychopath who is after me far behind.

Except... he's managed to find me time and time again over the last few years. I've moved four times, purchasing homes under different aliases, but he somehow hunts me down. Threatening notes followed by flowing love letters. And either bouquets of flowers at my house's gated entry or decapitated squirrels, depending on his mood. It was sporadic enough I'd sometimes get a false sense of security—thinking he'd gotten bored and moved on—but something else would always happen.

But he'd never broken into my home before.

I knew it was *him*, though.

My stalker.

He managed to cut the power, which alerted me something might be wrong. When I heard glass break near the back patio, I dialed 9-1-1 in a nanosecond and raced toward the panic room. Even though he cut the power, my security system had a battery backup. I'd known a silent alarm would be ringing somewhere, hopefully notifying the police.

It was a good thing, too, because the man took me down in the hallway just mere feet from the door to the panic room and before 9-1-1 could even answer my call. My only saving grace had been the security company alerting the police and a cruiser just blocks from my house. The wailing sirens as they converged on my house caused him to run. Thank God, because I'd been awfully close to losing consciousness from his hands locked around my throat.

I drop my fingers away from the bruising, but Rachel's gaze goes there, surveying the marks he left behind. When she looks at me, her eyes harden. "Kynan will protect you. We'll figure out who this shithead is, and he won't bother you anymore when we're done with him."

I manage a tremulous smile. "That's the most reassuring thing I've heard in a long time. The police haven't been able to do much with what little information they had over the last few years."

Her eyes go soft and almost apologetic. "I don't know the details of what happened between you and Kynan, but I've got the general gist of things."

A blush blazes through me, and I drop my gaze to my lap. "He hates me. I could hear it on the phone."

"I have no clue if that's true," she remarks simply. "But don't expect him to be nice. If you want him for this job, you should be ready to deal with his attitude."

I nod, acknowledging what she hadn't needed to reiterate. Kynan and I split ways twelve years ago, and it hadn't been pretty at all. I'd loved him so much. There had been a time when he'd been my entire world and sole future. But then I found out the worst about him, and it hurt too much to stay. So I left him behind without a backward glance. Leaving him is perhaps my greatest regret in life, but that doesn't make things any better for us right now.

Straightening, I meet Rachel's eyes. "I know exactly how Kynan feels about me. Yet, I'm still here. He's the one for this job."

"Why?" she asks, tilting her head in question. "There are a lot of other great security firms out there."

That's true. I've researched them over the years since the stalking started. Even used a few for personal security services. I could easily use the same ones again.

I curve my lips into a sardonic smile. "No matter his

feelings toward me, Kynan is a man of integrity. He'll take this far more seriously than anyone else would. I trust him."

"All right then," she says, then grabs the handle to her door and opens it. "Let's go on in."

I follow Rachel up the sidewalk, which is flush with cacti and tropical plants. Even though it's June in Vegas, I pull the sides of my zip hoodie around me for protection. I'm not looking my best, that's for sure. After I refused an ambulance to the hospital, I gladly accepted a police officer's offer for a ride straight to the airport. I'd thrown on some yoga pants, a tank top, and grabbed my hoodie from the closet. I was so eager to leave the area I didn't bring anything else other than my purse. I have no makeup on, my hair is a rat's nest, and I don't even have a brush because I don't carry one in my purse. No, I wouldn't do something as sensible as that. In addition to my purse, I usually always brought with me a huge cosmetic/vanity bag, which carried all the essentials needed to make sure I always look glamorous. Never even thought to bring that with me because my only thought was getting out of Santa Barbara and to Kynan for help.

There was never any doubt of where I'd go once I approached the ticket agent at the airport. The police officer kindly came in with me, and he stayed by my side until I made it to the security line. Still, I didn't stop looking over my shoulder until I was on the plane to Vegas and every last passenger had boarded. My life was now one led by fear and survival instinct, and I knew I couldn't survive it alone.

To my surprise, we get to Kynan's front door and Rachel punches in a security code to unlock it. She pushes it open, then motions me inside.

The splendor of his house is lost on me—not because I'm immune to opulence, but because it's not important to me. Over the years, many things I'd thought were important just aren't anymore.

Crossing my arms over my chest, I scan around with minimal curiosity. Mostly, though, all I feel is nervousness over seeing the man I once loved who now hates me.

Rachel shuts the door, and I follow her into the open living room with a view of a spacious veranda. It's filled with potted plants, a huge grill, and high-end furniture, but I barely take it in.

The sound of a door opening above catches my attention. I sweep my gaze up the massive, curved staircase that sits between the foyer and living area. There's laughter—both male and female—and then Kynan appears with a ravishingly beautiful woman wearing nothing but a short, silky robe. It's tied so loosely at her waist that her breasts are bared. His arm around her waist, he's whispering something in her ear that causes her to giggle again as they descend the staircase. Kynan's wearing track pants and a t-shirt. His dark blond hair is mussy. It's clear they just rolled out of bed.

The first time I see him in twelve years, my only thought is about how time has been damn good to him. His hair is worn the same way, along with his trademark facial hair that hovers somewhere between a short beard and a five o'clock shadow. Clearly, he takes his health seriously as his body is as buff and cut as it was when he was twenty-six. Those arms, sleeved with tattoos, were always my weakness. Apparently, they still are because I stare at them too long.

My face flushes with embarrassment over being in Kynan's home, unannounced and clearly ruining an evening with his girlfriend. Even worse is that I continue to ogle him shamelessly.

When he reaches the bottom of the stairs, his eyes come to me, but they linger only briefly and without a flicker of emotion before he addresses Rachel. "I don't need anything else tonight, Rach. Get home to Bodie and Tony."

Rachel inclines her head, then gives me a last reassuring smile that misses the mark with me. "See you later, Joslyn."

"Bye," I whisper, my throat feeling extremely parched from nerves and still raw from last night's attack.

When the door closes behind Rachel, Kynan drops his hand to the woman's ass and squeezes. "Be a love and get me a club soda from the bar."

That damn British accent is still sexy as hell, too, and I hope there's not going to be a lot of conversation tonight. I'm in sensory overload.

"Not another scotch?" the woman purrs with her hand to his chest as she leans into him.

He shakes his head, then glances at me. "Want something to drink?"

"I'm good."

Kynan's eyes dip briefly to my throat. He'd have to be blind not to notice the bruising, but I don't see so much as a facial tick from him. His expression stays as bland as unbuttered grits.

The redhead sashays off, neither bothering to make any introductions. Briefly, I watch her swaying hips while she makes her way over to a recessed wet bar built into one wall before I turn back to Kynan. I swallow to wet my throat. "I'm sorry. I shouldn't be barging in like this and interrupting your time with your girlfriend. I can go to a hotel, and we can meet in your office tomorrow."

Both Kynan and the woman give simultaneous snorts of amusement, but she's the one who responds. "Oh, I'm not his girlfriend."

Confused, I look back and forth between them.

Kynan just shrugs. "We met this afternoon."

"Oh," I say softly, the implication hitting me. I'm

not shocked over a one-night stand because there's nothing wrong with a little fun, but why in the world did he have Rachel bring me here?

"We met at The Wicked Horse," the woman adds conversationally. "I was getting flogged in the stocks, and Kynan rescued me. Whisked me off to this luxurious mansion for an evening of fun."

I blink stupidly, trying to process the strange sentences. "I'm sorry. The Wicked Horse?"

"It's a sex club I belong to," Kynan replies offhandedly on his way to a sumptuous-looking armchair. He drops down with elegant grace, then motions toward the couch to indicate I should take a seat.

Now I'm shocked. So much so I'm rooted to the spot. "Sex club?"

"Oh, don't sound so boorish, Joslyn," Kynan chastises in that godforsaken hot British accent. "You should give kink a try. You would have no shortage of movie stars and rock gods lining up for you."

Heat creeps up my neck, and I'm rendered speechless. A glass of club soda in her hand, the woman saunters over to Kynan. She settles right on his lap. When his hand goes between her legs, my entire body freezes.

And I don't mean to squeeze her thigh or give her a quick caress.

Nope, he slides it right to her core. While the hem of

her robe covers what he's doing, it's obvious it must feel good because her eyes roll back in her head, which then lolls on his shoulder. Her legs begin to fall open, obviously wanting to give him better access. I jerk my eyes to his face just in time to catch his smirk as he watches me closely for a reaction.

I spin away, mortified and equally pissed off. It's clear he's intentionally doing this to make me uncomfortable. I start for the door, unwilling to stand for whatever he's trying to prove.

"Stay," he commands and for a moment, I almost obey him. That voice of his... all cultured but incredibly arrogant and demanding. I used to obey him a lot when it came to sex, but I chalk that up to the fact I was just oh so young when we were together.

I'm not young and naïve anymore, so I keep walking.

I make it to the foyer before he calls out, "Walk out that door, Joslyn, and you know your life is in danger. Your psychopath could be out there right now."

They are the right words.

I freeze, feeling my shoulders slump in resignation and complete helplessness. Tears prick at my eyes, and I furiously blink them back.

Resignation fills me. Not only am I in a no-win situation right now, but I'm also going to have to accept I'll be forced to pay more than just money to get Kynan's help. As a means to make me repent for the wrongs he perceives I did to him, it's obvious he's going to humiliate me first by making me stay while he gets the woman off.

But to my surprise, he addresses the woman, "We're going to need to call it a night, love. Go get your clothes on, then call yourself a cab or an Uber. I've got some money in my wallet to pay for it. It's on the dresser."

"Sure thing," she replies. After, there's only the sound of kissing, moaning, and a deep groan from Kynan. I can only imagine what she's doing to him, but I refuse to turn around.

Only when I hear the woman's soft steps on the staircase do I give my attention to Kynan again.

"Take a seat," he says with a nod at the couch.

My walk is slow and measured. There's a slight limp I can't quite cover up because I banged my knee so hard when I was tackled to the floor last night. My entire body is covered in bruises from the fight that ensued as he tried to roll me over. I thought he was going to rape me, but he merely put his hands around my throat and started to choke the life out of me.

When I reach the couch, I sit awkwardly on the edge of the cushion with my hands clenched tightly on my lap, head down.

"Tell me everything," he says.

Raising my head, I face the man I used to love with every breath in my body.

And then I do just as he commands.

CHAPTER 3

Kynan

I FLIP THE bacon, glancing up from my efforts to look across the kitchen, through the living room, and to the curved staircase that leads to the second floor where Joslyn is still apparently sleeping. I had hoped the smell of food would lure her down, since I don't relish the thought of having to wake her up. Even the thought of hearing her husky morning voice or seeing her hair mussed from a long night's sleep would bring back too many unsolicited memories of when we were a couple.

Besides, it's still super early yet. I get up at five every morning to get in a quick workout, followed by breakfast and coffee. I'm on my third cup now. My stomach is growling because I've delayed starting to cook by at least an hour to give Joslyn an opportunity to get some more sleep. She looked bad last night, and she needs the rest.

Just the thought of those marks on her causes fury to swirl within me and I try to push it right back down again. I've got no business being enraged on Joslyn's behalf. She's nothing but a client to me now. I should only feel a healthy amount of concern for her safety with a pressing need for due diligence to catch this creepy fuck as soon as possible.

That's it.

Truthfully, she deserves nothing more from me than a professional job well done.

It's true that once, a long time ago, she had my love and undying devotion, but that was summarily killed when she left me with no explanation and moved to another state to pursue her career. One might think that's a little harsh of me, because shouldn't she be able to chase her dreams? And the answer is hell yes. But I'd offered to give up my career to follow her wherever her career might take her, so it was extra crushing when I wasn't invited along.

The object of my current ire comes down the stairs, and I hate how much I'm attracted to her as she carefully descends by supporting herself with one hand on the banister. She's now two days post attack from the stalker who managed to break into her house, and I can tell she's even more sore today than yesterday.

Despite everything, she's a goddamned punch to the gut. Joslyn is even more beautiful now than she was twelve years ago at the age of nineteen. She's filled out in all the right places and despite the haunted expression in her blue eyes, her face is a work of art any man would be hard pressed to ignore. Her hair is more of a platinum blonde than when we were together, a color I can only describe as silver moonlight. Granted, it could use a good brushing, but I find the pale color suits her even better except it makes the bruising on her neck stand out in stark contrast.

Those marks, clearly from a man's hands around her throat, were the first thing I noticed when I laid eyes on her last night. I'd battled a rage so intense I'd almost stumbled down the last two steps when I came down to meet her.

I've seen Joslyn a bunch of times over the years.

Usually on entertainment shows, giving interviews and such.

Accepting awards and signing autographs.

She's come a long way from her early days as a Vegas pop singer.

Even in a wrinkled t-shirt and threadbare sweatpants, she takes my breath away. Her hair is piled messily on top of her head like a shining halo. But I have to remember that she's no angel.

I pull the bacon from the pan, placing the slices on a paper-towel-lined plate. It gives me a reason to avert my eyes from Joslyn as she gingerly makes her way into the kitchen.

"Good morning," she says hesitantly.

"Morning," I reply, turning to give her a critical once over. I push aside the flutter in my stomach, which she somehow still makes me feel, then notice the bruising on her neck is a darker purple. I'm certain about one thing… before all this is through, I'm going to make that fucker pay for what he did to her. "Coffee?"

"I can get it," she replies with a wan smile. I nod toward the coffee pot on the back counter beside the sink. My eyes follow her as she makes her way around the island.

"Cups are in the cabinet above the pot and cream is in the fridge. Still take your eggs over easy?"

Joslyn jerks, glancing over her shoulder in surprise. "Yes. That's fine, or whatever's easiest."

"One's just as easy as the other." I shrug, hating I still remember something as simple as the way she eats her eggs after twelve years. I've tried extremely hard to forget everything about her.

Returning my attention to breakfast, I pull a clean pan from a cupboard and spray it with oil, setting it over a new flame on my six-burner range. I don't offer up conversation as Joslyn makes her coffee. When she takes a seat on a stool at the island, it puts her just in my peripheral vision. Staying silent, I crack eggs into the skillet.

"I want to apologize again for intruding last night," she offers me in a quiet voice. "I should have waited until we could meet at your office today."

"You weren't intruding," I reply. It's not said as a

means to soothe her conscience but to set up a jab that's meant to hurt. "I'd already fucked her. My evening was complete."

When Joslyn flinches, I feel like shit for being so bloody crass, but I'm trying to reconcile the anger over how she left me with the fury over the fact someone tried to kill her.

Fuck, I hate she still matters to me when I know she shouldn't.

Twelve years ago, I fell in love with Joslyn Meyers with no more effort than it takes to blow a feather into the air. I had just come to work for Jerico at his newly formed security service. We had served in Afghanistan together—Jerico with the U.S. Marines, while I'd been with the Royal Marines—and I was the first person he asked to join him on this private venture away from the military.

Jerico had warned me. He'd seen the way I watched her while she performed on stage in a popular Vegas pop act, and he'd told me to steer clear.

But I hadn't.

I couldn't.

And I had thought Joslyn felt the same. Granted, she was so young—not even twenty—and I wasn't much more mature at twenty-six, but it felt like the real deal to me.

I guess that's why it had hurt so much when she'd

broken it off with absolutely no forewarning it was coming. One day, we were head over heels in love. The next, she'd told me it was over and she was moving to Hollywood.

End of story.

I'm fairly sure I hated her then for making a tough guy like me hurt. For choosing a life without me. I hadn't known such a wisp of a girl could cause a physical pain inside my chest, but fuck if it didn't take me a long damn time to get over her.

The security panel in the short hallway to the laundry room chimes. A mechanical female voice drones out, "Warning... front door opened."

Joslyn jolts, a flash of fear crossing her face. My initial instinct is to gather her in my arms to soothe the terror away. Instead, I only say, "That's just Rachel."

As if on cue, Rachel enters the kitchen, carrying a box of donuts in one hand and a small duffel bag in another. "Good morning."

"Morning," Joslyn replies softly with a shy smile.

Rachel sets the duffel bag on the floor near Joslyn's stool. "Got you a travel bag with some clothes and toiletries."

"Thank you." Joslyn's tone is surprised and overly grateful.

I cock an eyebrow at the sweet confections in Rachel's hands. "Those things will kill you, Rach."

"But I'll go with a smile on my face," she teases with a grin, then tosses the box onto the island countertop in front of Joslyn. She opens the top, pulls out two donuts, and then nabs a paper towel. To Joslyn, she says, "Help yourself."

I slide Joslyn's over-easy eggs onto a clean plate, then toss a few slices of bacon on it. She ignores the donuts, giving me a barely perceptible, "Thank you," when I set the food in front of her. I'm sure I've set the atmosphere for her meek and quiet attitude right now, and that's fine.

Rachel and I need to settle some things, which is why I invited her over this morning.

"What's the plan?" she asks as she settles on a stool next to Joslyn.

I whisk more eggs in a bowl while I give Rachel the low down on what Joslyn and I talked about last night.

"Her stalker is incredibly smart," I reply, shooting a quick glance at Joslyn. She's now warily watching me just from the mention of this asswipe. "He's been able to find out where she lives, despite her using a protective alias to purchase her home. It tells me he might be a hacker—and a damned good one at that. I'd be shocked if he didn't already know she's here in Vegas."

Rachel nods in understanding. "Good thing you're going to spring Bebe."

Joslyn frowns. "Spring Bebe? What does that mean?"

"Just that we hopefully have our own hacker coming on board with Jameson soon," I reply, pouring my eggs into the skillet for a slow scramble. Giving my attention to Rachel, I continue with my initial analysis of our situation. "But just because he's smart doesn't mean he's not psycho. He's been pursuing her for almost two years now, with his ultimate fantasy being to kill her. Those dark thoughts don't just go away, so we have to expect him to come after her again."

"But when?" Rachel muses.

"Hopefully not long," I answer as I stir my eggs. "But he might be a little spooked at almost getting caught by the police, so I have an idea."

Both women give me their full attention. I look up from my cooking, my gaze centering on Rachel only. "We're going to bait him to come after Joslyn. Going to open the door figuratively to make it impossible for him to stay outside."

Joslyn gasps. "You want him to come after me?"

"He won't get near you."

"Can you guarantee that?" Her eyes are narrowed on me sharply.

"Yes," I say with a hard edge to my tone. There's no way I'd ever let that fucker touch a hair on her head ever again.

"How are you going to lure him?" Rachel asks, and I focus on her.

Pulling the pan from the flame, I scrape my eggs onto an awaiting plate, tossing some bacon on top. I'd given this a lot of thought after I'd shown Joslyn to a guest room last night. I turn the stove off, then put the pan back on it. Placing my hands on the edge of the counter, I lay out my plan to them.

"We're going to put on a show for him, and he won't be able to resist coming after Joslyn." I twist my neck slightly to give my full attention just to her. "We'll get your publicist on it. Announce you and I are a couple. We'll do a few photo ops. I'm going to brag how you're absolutely protected now under my watch and this loser isn't going to get anywhere near you. His ego won't be able to handle it. His psychosis will demand he prove me wrong."

"I've heard crazier ideas," Rachel says before taking a huge bite of a donut.

Joslyn, I notice, lets her gaze drift off so she's staring out the kitchen window into the side yard. Whether she's contemplating doubts or that I might be the craziest son of a bitch she's ever known, I have no clue. But while I might have all kinds of enmity for her, I don't want her to have the stress of worrying about this. I wouldn't want that on any of my clients.

"I'll keep you safe, Jos," I promise, surprised by the way I've so easily slipped back into using the endearment by shortening her name.

Those blue eyes come back to me and she nods. "I know. I trust you."

"Good," I say with a nod of my head, then turn back to Rachel. "I'll keep my current schedule. Joslyn will come with me to Pittsburgh and after I finish the interview, we'll head to her house on the West Coast where we'll start to set the trap."

"Pittsburgh?" Joslyn asks with surprise.

"Opening a new headquarters there, and I've got a potential employee to interview," is all I say. She's on a need to know basis and she doesn't need to know any more. Certainly not any details about my life and this amazing career I'm still building into something more involved and complex.

She doesn't deserve to know anything about my life, so I can't figure out why I'm all of a sudden frustrated when she doesn't press me about it. Instead, she just nods and picks up a piece of bacon to nibble on. It's disconcerting because the Joslyn I'd known was a firecracker. Her personality shone through at all times, and she never just sat by quietly while things unfolded.

I let it go, though, turning back to Rachel. "Going to need you to get a few things rolling for me."

"Shoot," she says, and I proceed to lay out the details of my plan to take this fucker down.

Then Joslyn can be on her way to a happy life and I can get back to my own.

CHAPTER 4

Joslyn

I'VE BEEN TO Pittsburgh a handful of times, usually a quick in and out for a show or concert. But it never fails to dazzle when I enter the city from the Fort Pitt tunnel. Before then, it was just a drive on a lazily curving interstate through the mountains and rolling hills.

Then it's a drive through the belly of a mountain before emerging onto the Fort Pitt bridge. It's a yellow steel, double-decked arched bridge that crosses the Monongahela River and heads straight for the heart of the city.

What makes this entrance into Pittsburgh so dramatic is when people come out of the tunnel, it's like boom... there's this sudden appearance of a beautiful city of tall glass and steel buildings surrounded by sparkling water. It's just something no one expects.

Kynan navigates the traffic with ease, telling me he's spent some time in this area. He has one hand resting casually on top of the wheel, the other on his left thigh where he taps his fingers to the beat of the music playing from the radio. He turned it on as soon as we pulled out of the airport, then turned the volume up enough to discourage conversation.

I don't mind because I've found it difficult and awkward to talk to him anyway. He's been cool and aloof today, spending this morning plotting with Rachel at the kitchen island while I went and took a shower.

An hour after that, we were at the private terminal at McCarran International Airport just outside of Vegas and Kynan was loading me onto a Lear jet bound for Pittsburgh. When I asked him why we weren't flying commercial, he merely said, "I want to make it hard for your stalker to track you."

That made me have a million other questions. *Why does he think he might still be tracking me right now? How long will we be in Pittsburgh? Is Kynan going to stay mad at me forever?*

None were asked because Kynan put on a pair of headphones when we settled into sumptuous leather captain's chairs on board the plane and promptly went to sleep.

We move deeper into the city, crossing another bridge. Pittsburgh sits at the confluence of the Allegheny and Monongahela rivers where they form the Ohio River. While the city was once known for its steel manufacturing, it's a leader in banking and medicine these days.

As Kynan cuts across city blocks, I notice the buildings become a bit shabbier and the streets more littered. Business people walking the streets give way to the homeless and aimless. I watch a drug purchase go down on a street corner as we wait at a red light. The next block down, a prostitute waves at Kynan as we drive by. If Kynan weren't the one sitting beside me, I'd be feeling decidedly unsafe to be in this part of the city by myself. I have to wonder where he's taking me.

At the next intersection, Kynan turns right and then immediately signals another right-hand turn. He pulls up to what appears to be basement parking under an old warehouse that runs the length of the entire block. It's four-stories high, not counting the parking level with graffiti sprayed over the red-brick surface. There are beautiful arched windows on every floor that must let in spectacular light if they weren't coated in so much grime.

There's a rolling metal gate closing off the entrance, but it rumbles open when Kynan taps something on his iPhone, presumably a security app. When he pulls in, I glance over my shoulder to see the gate rolling closed.

Kynan drives deep into the underground lot and parks the SUV near a stairwell, also covered in graffiti. I don't wait for him to open my car door, preferring to step out on my own. I'm immediately feeling insecure as only half the lights seem to be working and no natural light from the entrance reaches this far back. Kynan moves to the stairwell door. I quickly move to catch up with him, finally voicing my fear-tinged curiosity.

"Where are we?" I ask as we move up the flight of stairs.

"Welcome to the Jameson Pittsburgh office," he replies at the landing to the first floor. There's an old dusty wall sconce that barely provides enough illumination to reveal a faded numeral one painted on the heavy steel door.

"A real fixer-upper," I mutter as he punches a code in an alarm panel on the wall.

A panel that appears incredibly new and high tech, a sharp contrast to the overall dilapidation of the building. A short chime sounds, and I can hear a lever inside the steel door click.

Kynan pushes the handle down, pulls the door open, and motions for me to precede him inside. It's what I'd imagine an abandoned warehouse would look like. Empty floor space of approximately ten thousand square feet. There's a thick layer of dust on the cement floor and scattered trash all about, indicating this building has been sitting empty for quite some time. I wonder what it was used for.

We move across the space to the opposite side where I notice a freight elevator. It's got a metal gate Kynan opens and I step inside. He follows and hits a button for the second floor, closing the metal gate behind him. We take off with a slight lurch and a groan of cables, slowly rising upward. I expect to see another similar floor, but as the second floor comes into view, my jaw drops wide at what I'm seeing. I think this is what Dorothy must have felt when she stepped foot into the full-blown color of Oz for the first time.

Before me is a completely finished and renovated office space. Kynan opens the gate and I step onto glossy, hardwood floors in a brown so deep it almost looks black. The perimeter walls are the same red brick as the outside of the building, but it's been sand blasted and restored to its original glory. Above me are exposed iron pipes, steel beams, and black ductwork, lending an industrial vibe to the space but the furnishings are elegant and expensive. Black leather couches and chairs dot the area with silver aluminum tables holding uniquely different lamps. A bold steel gray rug sits under the furniture, lending a warm feel to the entire space, and a massive painting of galloping ghostly white horses on a black backdrop covers one wall.

In the middle of the room is a wide, floating staircase that ascends to the next level and to the levels beyond that from what I can see. It's made of black iron and reclaimed wood with steel cables for support.

"Wow," is all I can say as I look around in shock at the upscale space that stands in sharp contrast to the crappy exterior and first floor.

Past the staircase, the open space is punctuated with red brick support columns. In between those sit simple black desks with mesh office chairs. Each desk has a computer screen, phone, and printer. On the back wall sits a row of glassed-in offices with black metal frames, each one empty of any furnishings except the middle one. It's larger than the others to either side. Inside sits a long oval conference table. I follow him in there, marveling at the artistry as the table sits on heavy twisted beams of rusted steel—perhaps a nod to Pittsburgh's heritage and history—with a long rectangular slab of gray, speckled cement on top. It's sturdy, masculine, and imposing, everything that describes Kynan and Jameson Force Security.

The room itself is barren other than the table and chairs, the only warmth coming from the three large arched windows that run floor to ceiling. The outside is so coated with dust and dirt I can't see what's on the other side, but they're beautiful, nonetheless.

"If these are your offices, how come you've only restored this floor and by the looks of it, the ones above?" I ask Kynan curiously.

"Have a seat," Kynan says, pointing specifically to a chair. I take it, and he sits two down from me at the end of the table, a position of authority. I get the distinct impression he wants to talk now. But thankfully, he appeases my inquisitiveness first. "These offices are sort of 'off the books'. It's where our more covert type of operations will be based from, which includes top-secret government work. It's not open to the general public or even potential visiting customers. Only employees of Jameson. I'd like to keep up the appearance this is just an abandoned old building."

"What's above us?" I ask, since he's in a sharing mood.

"Third floor is all tech and weapons support, including a soundproof shooting range. Fourth floor is going to be communal space... kitchen, gym, living room, theater, and dining room."

"Communal space?"

"For any agents who want to live here. We're also upfitting five personal apartments on the fourth floor. Call it a perk of the job."

"Will you be living here?"

"Yeah," he says, then shakes his head with exasperation. "As soon as they're ready to move in."

I have many more questions, mostly dealing with what type of operations he could possibly be doing that would require such a set up and secrecy on top of that. It fascinates me wondering what this man has made for himself. But I also know it's none of my business, and I doubt he's willing to indulge me.

So I merely fold my hands in my lap, letting my silence indicate he now has the floor for whatever we need to discuss.

"You and I are going to head out tomorrow morning for your house in California. We've got a stop to make along the way, but I need you to arrange to have your mom and whatever publicist you use—or whoever else is on your team these days—ready to meet with us early the day after."

My chin lifts. "My mom isn't managing me anymore."

Kynan blinks in surprise. "Since when?"

"For a long time," I murmur. "She's actually back in Cunningham Falls, married to a rancher."

Kynan just stares as he digests this, and I get why it's surprising to him. My mom, Madeline Meyers, was my manager when Kynan and I first met years ago. She's actually my stepmom but having raised me since I was six meant she was always just my mom. The woman who gave birth to me died in childbirth, so I don't remember her.

Why it's probably surprising was Madeline Meyers sole purpose in life was to make her daughter rich and famous. She was like a pit bull with my career, using a heavy hand to direct and control me at all times. Only after I'd met Kynan was I able to get a little of that control back, but that was rather short-lived. My mom never liked Kynan. She felt he was a distraction, which was why she'd had a tough time hiding her gloating smile when I found out he cheated on me. She so enjoyed showing me the picture of Kynan and another woman.

It was crushing being shown the man I had fallen in love with was seeing another woman behind my back. I couldn't defend against the physical evidence she showed me, and it made it extremely easy to run from Kynan. I cleanly broke things off, choosing not to confront him on his treachery. After a simple phone call to him, I merely ran off with my mom to Hollywood where I could start my career in earnest, without the distraction of young love.

"Do you have a manager? Publicist?" Kynan asks, and I jolt back to the present, ignoring the nauseated feeling produced by thinking about the comprehensive investigative report my mom gave me about Kynan. She'd hired someone to check him out. To tail him and make sure he was good enough for her daughter.

Turns out... he wasn't.

Strangely, twelve years later, I find myself without anger because I don't have room for it. I guess the passage of time makes it so I just don't care anymore about why Kynan would do that to me. Besides... I chose to leave without asking him those questions. It would serve no purpose now. On top of that, I'm terrified I'll be killed by some stalker and Kynan is my sole means of hope I'll get through this. I can't waste my energies on wondering about my past with him. I have to worry about my future and staying alive now.

I finally respond to his original question. "I have a manager and a publicist. You want them both there?"

"Yes," he replies, drumming his fingers on the table. "I want to discuss the best way to reveal us as a couple to the media. I'm thinking an engagement will do the most to piss your stalker off, but we'll have to massage a cover story since this is coming out of the blue. I suggest we stick as close to the truth as possible… that we've known each other for years and have reconnected. Sound okay?"

The thickness in my throat prevents me from answering right away. It got clogged with emotion when he said "engagement" since I'd once dreamed about having that with Kynan. I thought we'd be together forever, which meant getting married and having babies one day.

Now I'm stuck in this weird alternate universe. Someone is hunting me, and I have to pull off a fake relationship with the man I used to love and who broke my heart because I clearly wasn't enough for him.

I give a cough to clear my throat. "That's fine. I'll put calls in now."

"Good," he says, then he checks his watch. "You can hang out in here. I'm interviewing someone for a position at Jameson. They'll be here soon. Then we'll go check into a hotel for the evening."

"How long do you think this is going to last?" I ask.

"You mean before this guy will make a move on you?"

When I nod, Kynan's eyes turn hard. "Hopefully not long. I know it's not a comfortable situation for either of us."

"Agreed," I say softly. "But I do appreciate you doing this for me. I can't thank you enough."

"Thank me when we bring the guy down," he mutters before pushing up from his chair. "If you can, work on setting up that meeting for the day after tomorrow. My meeting shouldn't last more than half an hour."

"Got it," I reply, then pull my phone out of my purse.

I'm completely at Kynan's mercy. I can only hope this plan of his—while dangerous and scary—produces results quickly. It's just far too painful being near him and being reminded at the same time he was once the love of my life.

CHAPTER 5

Kynan

I LEAVE JOSLYN in the conference room to make my way back down to the first-floor entrance door. As expected, Cruce Britton is waiting there for me. I had given him the alarm code to the parking deck gate, which randomly changes every twenty minutes, but I wasn't going to give him full access to the building until I'd officially hired him. He still needed to pass personal muster with me, which was the reason for this meeting.

"Glad you could come," is how I greet him after I unlock the steel door and pull it wide. I offer my hand, and he gives it a crushing shake.

Cruce Britton is a big guy. He stands at six-foot-six. While I'll never admit it to him, he's my number-one recruit to join this new branch of Jameson.

"Got a real fixer-upper here," he says as he steps into the warehouse and looks around.

"You're not the first to say that." I laugh, thinking of Joslyn's words just a few minutes ago. "But not all is as it seems."

I take Cruce the same route I had just taken Joslyn, up through the freight elevator to the second floor. He whistles low through his teeth in appreciation as we step onto the second floor.

"Nice cover," he says as I lead him over to some black leather chairs where we can sit and talk. He notices Joslyn in the glass-walled conference room, where she paces back and forth with a phone to her ear. She's far enough away her details are fuzzy, but her platinum hair and slight build would have any man looking twice.

"Who's that?" Cruce asks as he thumbs her way.

"Client." I give her a glance, hating how even from far away she still causes my skin to tighten.

Cruce cocks one eyebrow at my clipped tone.

I force myself to relax, embarrassed the woman makes me so uptight. "She's got a stalker after her. He managed to break into her house, then tried to strangle her a few days ago."

Because Cruce is a man who has spent his entire career protecting people, I'm not surprised by the hardening of his jawline with immediate concern.

"Got any leads?" he asks.

Before I answer, I motion with my hand for him to take a chair and I take another perpendicular to him. He folds his muscular frame in with surprising grace.

"I'm taking her back to California tomorrow. We're going to try to lure him to come after her again."

"Risky."

"We'll be ready for him, and she'll be fully protected," I assure him. "It's low risk."

Cruce makes a sound low in his throat that sounds like disapproval to me. And I like it, because I don't need a team that thinks just like me. I want to consider all angles, and I've been looking forward to this interview with Cruce because it makes for an excellent opportunity to see how he thinks on his feet.

I ease into it, though.

"I have to say," I drawl casually as I cross one leg over the other. "You certainly have the best letter of recommendation I've ever seen."

Cruce chuckles, the corners of his eyes crinkling in amusement. "Can't really top the president of the United States writing a letter on your behalf, can you?"

"No, you can't," I agree.

Cruce Britton has spent his entire working career at the U.S. Secret Service. His resume gave me the bullet points. Bachelor's degree in criminal justice, eight years in the Los Angeles field investigative office, then four years protecting the newly sworn in Vice President Jonathan Alexander and his family.

When the president decided not to run for a second term due to health issues, Jonathan Alexander threw his hat into the ring and won an easy victory. He was sworn in three months ago as our country's newest president, yet Cruce is sitting here in search of a new job.

"Why didn't you take the presidential detail when Alexander took office?" I ask bluntly. "You spent four years protecting him as vice president. Based on the letter he gave me on your behalf, I'm guessing he wanted you by his side for the next four years."

Cruce smiles casually. "Actually... we're allowed to stay on protective detail only about five years. I'd already served four so, at best, I'd only have a year with him. It just seemed like an appropriate time to start a new career."

"What happens once you're off protective detail?" I ask curiously, since I don't know a lot about the Secret Service.

"Back to a field office doing investigations. Mostly financial crime and fraud. And no offense to those who do that shit, but I'm not a cop. Don't enjoy sitting behind a desk either."

I nod in understanding and empathy. One of the reasons I wanted to expand Jameson into more covert and dangerous stuff is I'm getting a little bored myself. Much of running this business is sitting behind a desk. For a self-proclaimed adrenaline junkie, it's not been my happiest times as the head of this company.

The Secret Service is not ordinarily where I'd recruit from for this new group I'm forming within Jameson. Sure, someone like Cruce is an incredible marksman and his attention to detail when it comes to protective services is unparalleled. He'd be a no brainer to put in Vegas with Rachel and let him protect high-profile celebrities.

But this new venture requires a bit more than that. Most of my recruits are going to be former Special Forces since I want their advanced fighting and weapons skills, knowledge of explosives, and actual battle experience, which means they're cool under pressure.

Ordinarily, I wouldn't have looked twice at someone applying from the Secret Service, but Cruce does have something that sets him apart from the rest of the organization.

"Tell me about the attempt on then Vice President Alexander's life," I say, and he blinks in surprise.

I watch him carefully to see if there's any reticence because I can't ever have one of my guys holding back on me.

He merely nods in understanding as to why I'd want to know more about it. After all, it made Cruce an international sensation and won him the undying gratitude of a soon-to-be president.

"There are a lot of details I can't give you," he begins by saying, and I don't bother telling him I've got high enough security clearance with both the U.S. and British governments I could get all the details if I wanted.

But I don't because I don't care. I just want to hear

him recount what happened, so I can I gauge just how traumatic it really was to him.

"Tell me what you can," I assure him.

Cruce's blue eyes—which are really an unusually light shade—darken quite a bit. His voice takes on an almost somber tone. "You know the set up... Jonathan Alexander—who was vice president at the time—was giving a graduation speech at Loyola, which is his alma mater. I was his primary and positioned off to his left, just behind him and the podium. When he finished the speech, I let him precede me off the stage and into the wings of the theater we were in. The plan was to take him straight to the limo waiting outside as he had a flight to catch. Two other agents were waiting by the double doors that led to the car."

Cruce falls silent. He takes a moment to rotate his neck, as if it had tightened up on him. I can faintly hear bones pop.

His gaze comes to me and locks. "I don't know how I saw it. I normally shouldn't have been watching for it. My job was to consider everything that could be a potential threat to Cavalier."

Cavalier being the code name the Secret Service used for the vice president. I press him to continue. "But you saw something."

"I just had a feeling," he says with a small shake of his head and a wry smile. "Don't ask me how or why, but I looked at Nicholson instead."

He was the Secret Service agent at the door. His name will be forever embedded in our history books as the man employed to protect the vice president and who also tried to kill him.

"It was a flash of silver, but it was shadowy. I couldn't really tell what it was," Cruce continues with a tone akin to amazement. "It could have been the silver wrapping on a stick of gum for all I knew, but my gut said it was something more sinister. I didn't hesitate."

No, he didn't. In front of a video crew who had been filming a documentary on Vice President Alexander—as it was widely known at that point he was going to make a run for president—Cruce Britton hadn't hesitated a moment in pulling out his service pistol and cranking four bullets into Special Agent Nicholson's chest.

It was all caught on film, so there was no misinterpreting what Nicholson had planned. From his pocket, he'd pulled an eight-inch shiv, raised it high in the air, and had started lunging at Vice President Alexander when the first bullet caught him in the chest. It all came out in the investigation, but Nicholson held a deep-seated grudge against the current administration for its foreign war policies. Plus, he was a little touched in the head. He had hoped to make a statement by killing the vice president, and he had fully intended to die for the cause. There was a letter in his breast pocket.

What made Cruce's actions so heroically phenomenal was it all went down in just a few seconds. He'd reacted on pure instinct. There hadn't been anything that ever could have led him to believe one of his own would try to kill the VP.

"There are some who believe you acted too rashly," I point out to Cruce. "That you had time to engage him in hand-to-hand combat to stop the attack, which would have saved his life."

That produces a chuckle out of Cruce, and his eyes actually lighten up and sparkle. "Only person's opinion who matters is Alexander's, and he's grateful for what I did."

"So no second guessing yourself?" I ask.

"Never," he assures me. "If he'd had a piece of gum in his hand, I'd be in prison suffering the consequences."

That's what I needed to hear. It's not up to me or anyone else to judge the situation. The case was thoroughly investigated by the Justice Department, and Cruce was cleared of any wrongdoing. In fact, he ended up getting a presidential commendation out of it. But I needed to know he was at peace with his decision to kill someone. It's not something I tend to doubt from my employees who are former Special Forces.

He's satisfied me on that front, and I want him at Jameson.

"The job is yours if you want it." I'd previously laid

out salary and benefits to him during a phone interview last week. He was interested in one of the new apartments upstairs. However, my offer to him was contingent on his references panning out—and a strong letter of praise from the current president suffices—and me meeting with him first. It's safe to say that as of this moment, I'm confident in opening the doors to him. "Only other thing you'd have to do is a psych evaluation."

"I'm okay with that. When would you want me to start?"

"Today if you want," I answer with a smile. "The apartments upstairs won't be ready for a few weeks, but I'll put you up in a hotel of your choice as part of your signing bonus."

"I'm definitely interested," he tells me, and I don't miss the almost sly tone of his voice. He leans forward in his chair, propping his elbows on his knees. "But I need something from you first."

Some would be offended, but I find myself intrigued. "What's that, mate?"

"I need a reference from you," he says bluntly. "A high-ranking member of congress would suffice, although I'd settle for someone at the CIA or Homeland Security. I want to know that what you plan to do here at Jameson isn't a pipe dream. I want to know Jameson is trusted by our government."

I just stare at Cruce, realizing if I land him on board with us, I've got a true leader on my hands. While he may have had no hesitation in pumping his colleague full of lead based on just a "flash of silver" and "gut instinct," he's not really the impetuous type as proven by his care in checking me out as thoroughly as I'm doing to him. That makes me want him on my team even more.

"I'll have three names for you to contact by tomorrow morning," I assure him as I stand from my chair.

He follows suit, and we shake hands. "You'll have my answer as soon as I check you out then," Cruce says with a smile.

"It will be 'yes'," I reply confidently, knowing he'll be impressed with how deep Jameson is already in with the U.S. government. Over the past decade, we've done quite a few off-the-books missions that saved lives, dollars, and reputations.

Cruce says he can see himself out of the building, and I don't feel the need to escort him. If I didn't trust him implicitly, I wouldn't have made the job offer.

I instead turn toward the conference room, noting Joslyn is now sitting in one of the chairs, head bent over her phone. When I open the door, she jolts slightly. There's no hiding the tiny bit of fear and panic I assume comes pretty naturally to a woman who has to be skittish as hell after what she's been through.

"Get everything set up for the meeting?" I ask.

"Breakfast meeting, day after tomorrow. At my house."

"Perfect," I reply, motioning for her to stand. "Let's head over to the hotel and get checked in for the night."

Joslyn looks exhausted. She's had a rough few days between someone trying to kill her, having to grovel to an ex she's on bad terms with so I'd take her case, and then flying cross country today. She's not going to fare any better tomorrow as we head back west, but if I can get a good meal into her and several hours of solid sleep, she shouldn't feel any worse.

CHAPTER 6

Joslyn

*H*IS HANDS CLOSE *around my throat, and my oxygen is immediately closed off. Although he's wearing a ski mask over his face, I know I'd be able to recognize him by the color of his eyes. A golden-yellow color shot through with streaks of brown. Some might consider them beautiful but not me. There's too much malice and hate within them to be considered anything but evil.*

Bending his head so his mouth hovers just above my own, he murmurs, "I know we're just getting started, but I can honestly say... you've been my favorite."

His hands tighten even harder, and I feel something pop in my throat as my world turns black.

I jolt awake, sitting up straight in bed and gasping for breath. My hands clutch at my throat, trying to pull his fingers away, but they come away with nothing. It takes a moment for it to permeate.

A dream.

Another fucking dream.

I flop on my pillows, which are damp with sweat,

and rub my hand over my face. "Shit," I mutter with a tiny laugh of relief that I'm alive and well.

It's the same dream I've had for the last three nights since that asshole attacked me in my own home. I dreaded even falling asleep tonight, knowing this night terror was probably going to happen again.

I take in a few deep breaths, willing myself to accept I'm safe and secure in a Pittsburgh hotel. I've got a man who was trained by the Special Forces in the other bedroom of this suite—one who is well armed. Besides, my stalker is most likely still on the West Coast. No matter how good he might be with computers, it's unlikely he's tracked me here given the private flight we took and registering under Kynan's name.

"You're safe, Joslyn," I murmur into the darkness right as my belly rumbles.

And hungry, apparently. I'd barely picked at the room service meal I'd ordered and eaten alone. Kynan had dinner down in the hotel restaurant as he had another potential employee to interview, but he assured me I was safe during his absence with an armed guard standing in the hallway outside the suite door. I didn't bother asking who. I just assumed it was one of his Jameson employees from Vegas or maybe even someone local. Regardless, the cost would be added to my bill, but that was okay.

I can afford to throw unlimited funds at securing my

safety, which is exactly what I intend to do. I've hired the best, and I've got no doubt Kynan will get the situation resolved for me.

My stomach gurgles again, and I roll off the bed. I pad quietly across the thick carpet, then open the door that leads into the main living area. It's dark with a few rays of moonlight slashing diagonally across the room. My gaze goes to Kynan's bedroom door, directly across from mine. It's opened several inches, but it's too dark to see anything inside. I assume he's sleeping, but something tells me probably not soundly. On my tiptoes, I make every effort to move in silence toward the refrigerator. I saw some trail mix in there earlier when I'd gotten a bottle of water.

I slide past the couch, around the end table, and make it to the fridge as quiet as a mouse. When I pull it open, it makes a slight hiss. Through the dim light that glows, I make out the glass cannister of trail mix. I barely have my fingers around it when I hear Kynan say from behind me, "Grab me a bottle of water, will you?"

Jumping, I squeak in surprise as my hand goes to my heart. I whip around to see him lying on the couch. Two rays of moonlight cut across his body, illuminating the black gun he has on his chest. He's fully clothed, even wearing his shoes.

"What are you doing? And why do you have your gun out?" I ask, scanning the darkened room before coming to rest on him.

Sighing, Kynan reaches an arm behind him to the lamp on the side table. The room floods with light, causing me to blink against the brightness. When I'm able to focus again, Kynan is rolling off the couch. He places the gun on the coffee table.

"Decided to sleep out here," he says to answer my question. Then he just stops and stares, his eyes running boldly down my body and moving up twice as slowly.

I blush from the tips of my toes to the roots of my hair when I remember what I'm wearing. I've got on a soft cotton camisole and a tiny pair of matching shorts. My nipples are hard as rocks and pushing against the fabric, and the fire in Kynan's eyes says he appreciates every bit of it.

I cross my arms quickly over my chest and Kynan brings his gaze back to my face. He's neither embarrassed nor chagrined to have been caught blatantly checking me out, but he also doesn't seem affected anymore. His tone is bland and uninterested. "Just doing my duty to protect you, Joslyn. If I'd been in that room with the door closed, wouldn't have done much good if someone had come sneaking in here, now would it?"

"You really think that's going to happen? Here in Pittsburgh?" I ask.

"Unlikely, but not impossible." Kynan nods toward the fridge, which is still open. "Hand me a water, would you?"

"Sure," I mumble, then turn to grab two bottles before closing the door.

When I hand one off to him, he moves to the couch, taking a seat on one edge. He twists the cap off and takes a sip before asking, "Why are you up?"

"Bad dream," I reply quietly, moving to take a seat on the other end of the couch. I hunch my shoulders inward, hoping to alleviate the pull of my camisole over my breasts, but Kynan's not paying them any attention anymore. His eyes are locked with mine.

"About your attack?" he asks.

"Yeah," I admit as I trace my finger down the edge of the water bottle. "The part where he was choking me and I was on the verge of passing out."

I don't expect sympathy from Kynan. He doesn't give it to me, either, but he does offer assurance. "That will never happen again, Joslyn. I promise you. You're safe."

I nod, thankful for his words. I trust him, but it still doesn't remove all the fear. "He said something to me... right before the police pulled into my driveway with the sirens blaring."

"What's that?"

"He said I'd been his favorite." I shudder as I force the words out.

Kynan blinks in surprise. "As if he'd done it before?"

SAWYER BENNETT

"That's the way I took it."

His eyebrows, much darker than the blond hair on his head, rise. "I'm assuming you told the police that."

"Of course," I reply, a little incensed he'd think I wouldn't. "I told them everything. Hell... I've been telling them everything. I've reported every creepy letter, flower arrangement, and dead squirrel he's ever left for me."

Heat flashes in Kynan's eyes, and there's not an ounce of sensuality to it. It's pure, blazing fury I'd been tormented that way. A wave of security sweeps over and wraps around me as I realize I finally have someone invested in my problem. I know, without a doubt, that hiring Kynan was the right decision no matter how much pain it dredged up.

"I've got a call into the lead detective on this," he says with a hard edge to his tone. "I'm going to find out everything they have and haven't done and then I'm going to fix your problem for you. Okay?"

"Thank you," is the best reply I have, but I'm so immensely grateful I can almost see a light at the end of what's been a very dark tunnel.

I take another sip before capping the water bottle. I start to unfold my legs, intent on going back to bed, but Kynan stops me cold me with his next words. "Why isn't your mom managing you anymore?"

Kynan wasn't overly fond of my mother's domineer-

58

ing ways when we were together, but I know without a doubt he understood her zeal to make me famous and didn't begrudge her love for me. Conversely, my mom was not Kynan's fan at all. Apparently, she was right.

Still, I eventually realized through the continued course of our complicated mom/daughter/celebrity/manager relationship that my mom's goals and mine weren't at all in alignment. While I can never repay her for the opportunities she secured for me, I will never deny I became a much happier woman once I cut her loose as my manager and insisted we have only a mother/daughter relationship.

"It just became too contentious," I answer after a bit of thought. How did I sum up all that complication, even if he was aware of some of it?

"She always wanted what was best for you," he says neutrally.

"Not always," I reply, unable to hide the slight tone of bitterness in my voice. But I'm also not about to lay every dirty detail before this man. He lost the right to know the personal details of my life when he cheated on me. "But it was the right decision to end that part of our relationship."

"I can't imagine she took that well."

I should get up and go to my bedroom. End the conversation. End this need inside of me to have a personal connection with this man.

Instead, my mouth opens and I blab a bit. "She didn't understand, and she was really hurt by what I did. She moved back to Cunningham Falls, and wouldn't speak to me for a few years."

Kynan makes a growling noise low in his throat, a clear indication he doesn't like my mother's actions. I didn't like them either. It hurt me she couldn't be happy just being my mom.

"But..." I continue, unable to hide the tremulous quaver in my words. "She started coming around. We've been able to repair most of the relationship over the years. It's helped she got remarried and has someone else to focus her attention on."

He stares for a long moment before he lifts his chin, giving a short motion toward my bedroom door. "You should try to get back to sleep. We've got to get up in just a few hours to head to the airport."

"Where are we going?" I ask. He'd said we had a stop to make on the way to California.

"Fort Worth," he replies.

"Texas?"

"The one and only." He gestures again toward my bedroom. "Go get some sleep. We have a long day tomorrow."

I'm not in the least bit tired—even still a little afraid to go back to sleep, worried my nightmare will resume again. But I push off the couch and walk away from the first genuine conversation I've been able to have with Kynan since we've reunited. I hate to admit it... but it felt good talking to him.

Too damn good.

CHAPTER 7

Kynan

THERE'S ONLY ONE federal super max prison in the United States, and it's housed in Florence, Colorado. It holds the most violent offenders as well as those who pose a risk to national security. Timothy McVeigh, Theodore Kaczynski, and Robert Hanssen are just a few of the celebrity inmates who have been housed there.

It's the perfect place to keep a prisoner such as Bebe Grimshaw, except for the fact Bebe is a woman. As such, she was placed at the Federal Medical Center in Fort Worth, Texas. It's a federal prison for females of all security levels, including those with mental and physical health needs, and it sits in the northeast corner of the Naval Air Station Joint Reserve Base in Fort Worth.

Bebe has no special needs, but she is a high national security risk. For the last seven years she's called FMC Carswell her home, she's been in solitary confinement. That means for twenty-three hours a day, she's in a single inmate cell. She's allowed outside in the yard for one hour a day, and she's not allowed access to the prison library due to the nature of her crimes. By all accounts, seven years of solitary would be enough to drive anyone mad, but the warden gave me her file and it seems to indicate she's been a pretty stable and model prisoner.

Still, I don't have the skills necessary to make that determination, which is why I arranged for Dr. Corinne Ellery to meet me at the prison today. She's doing the psych evaluations I require for the people I'm bringing aboard Jameson Force Security. Currently, she's flipping through Bebe's file while we wait for the guards to bring her in to meet us.

I had thought about leaving Joslyn on the plane while I drove to the prison to see Bebe Grimshaw, but it didn't feel right leaving her behind. Not that I had much worry her stalker could have tracked her to Fort Worth from Pittsburgh and arranged to arrive there himself, not with having to bypass the private terminal security and breeching the plane that was protected by an armed guard.

I just didn't want her to be alone.

So here she sits in a small room with a metal table bolted to the floor and four flimsy plastic chairs. Surprisingly, she hasn't asked why we're here. Quietly, and without any curiosity, she accepted my statement we had to stop in Texas to visit a prison as we boarded the plane this morning.

Frankly, she hasn't said much of anything since we

left the Jameson offices yesterday. I checked us into a two-bedroom suite at the Omni William Penn, but ended up sleeping on the couch in the main living area that separated the two rooms. I did this with my gun resting on my stomach because while I doubted her stalker had those types of resources, I wasn't going to take things lightly. It was a miserable night of sleep, mainly because Joslyn tiptoed out of her room around one and raided the fridge for a snack. I don't know if she saw me on the couch, but damn if I didn't see all of her illuminated from the moon rays filtering in through the window. Her hair was bunched on top of her head, and she was in nothing but a thin tank and shorts that barely covered her ass. My body reacted, and I hated myself for it. At thirty-eight, I would have hoped to have a little more control of myself, but Joslyn Meyers is an irresistible siren. While my heart and brain have disconnected from her, it appears my cock has not.

"I'm not sure this is a good idea," Dr. Ellery says as she closes the thick folder that holds everything known about Bebe Grimshaw. "The effects of seven years in solitary are incredibly unpredictable. Plus, Kynan... she's an admitted felon who did some very bad things."

"Which is why I have you here now," I reply smoothly as I pull the file across the table. "To figure out if she's redeemable."

My eyes cut to Joslyn sitting to my right, and I don't

see a single question in her gaze. I mean, she must have figured out we're here to meet a prisoner, but she doesn't seem to give two fucks as to why. I know this is because I've done nothing to foster an open environment for communication, but it's not every day someone gets unfettered access inside a federal prison to an incredibly notorious criminal mastermind.

I flip the folder open and survey the picture of Bebe Grimshaw. It was her mug shot when she was arrested by the FBI. She was young... twenty-two. Bleached-blonde hair cut short and spiky. Fake diamond stud in her nose, a ring through her lip, and a barbell through her eyebrow. Her booking sheet describes multiple tattoos over her arms, ribs, back, and legs. If I flip through the folder more, I'll find photos of everyone for documentation. I've read the contents of this folder three times, provided to me by a friendly US Congressman. I totally understand Dr. Ellery's reservations, but I've got a hunch.

There's a loud buzzing sound outside the door, then the heavy slide of metal as it's unlocked. Joslyn, her back to the door, twists in her seat as we all watch it swing open. Bebe Grimshaw shuffles in with shackles on her thin wrists and ankles, locked together by an intermediary chain. Gone is the short, blond hair. Her natural color is a lustrous bluish-black that even prison hasn't dulled over the years. It's long and braided in the back.

Her frame is slight beneath her prison uniform of a khaki button-up shirt and loose pants with white slip-on tennis shoes. She resembles a delicate fairy who got stuck in burlap.

Bebe scans her three visitors, her eyes hard and suspicious. She has no clue why she's been summoned here, but I can also see she's slightly curious. I was told she only gets two visitors twice a year. Past that, she has no connections to the outside world.

A guard comes in behind Bebe and unlocks her shackles. He gathers them up and exits, pulling the door closed behind him.

I stand from the table, then offer my hand to her. "Hi, Bebe. My name is Kynan McGrath."

She shakes my hand, still regarding me with general distrust. I nod at Corinne. "That's Dr. Ellery. She's a psychiatrist."

At this, Bebe blinks in surprise, but then she gestures at Joslyn. "And why is Joslyn Meyers sitting in a prison room with me?"

Not surprised she knows who Joslyn is. Most anyone who has access to TV does. She's not only an award-winning pop star, but she's also an accomplished actress. While Bebe is denied access to the library and internet, she has been allowed a small TV in her 4x9 cell that only gets four channels, but those include major networks, so it makes sense she's seen something with Joslyn in it over the years.

"She's a client of mine," I reply, sweeping a hand toward the empty chair. "Why don't you take a seat?"

Bebe shuffles around the table, walking as if still shackled. I'm guessing it's a product of habit and having little space within which to maneuver. She sits slowly and puts her clasped hands on the table, her eyes locking on mine. "What can I do for you, Mr. McGrath?"

"I'd like to offer you a job." It's said bluntly, and Joslyn jerks in her seat. Dr. Ellery shakes her head over my rash proclamation, but Bebe merely cocks an eyebrow.

"You'll have to wait thirteen more years before I'm supposedly eligible for parole," Bebe drawls with an amused smile, and it's clear she isn't taking me seriously.

"I can get you paroled today," I say firmly, and her smile freezes before it slides away.

"No one has that type of power," she replies tightly.

"I do." I give her a charming grin. "But before I work my magic, I need you to tell me something. Why did you get caught?"

Bebe's eyes widen in surprise, not over my assertion I can spring her from prison, but that I'd even care to know why she landed here in the first place.

Not "how" but "why," and that's a particularly important distinction in my mind. Bebe's eyes cut to Dr. Ellery, who gives her an encouraging smile. They then drift to Joslyn, who now seems to be invested in this conversation. She leans forward slightly in her chair as she watches Bebe carefully.

When Bebe focuses on me again, I can see something warring deep in her eyes. I don't need Dr. Ellery's formal professional opinion to know Bebe isn't a trusting individual, so I decide to help her along the way.

I begin by explaining all about Bebe Grimshaw. "Bebe is incredibly intelligent. She turned down scholarships from prestigious colleges and universities all over the world, choosing to go to MIT, where she studied computer science. In her sophomore year, she got pregnant. While I can't tell from her file if it was a love match, the father didn't stick around. By Bebe's junior year, she was a single mother struggling to raise a son on her own while continuing her schooling."

I dare not look at Bebe, but I can actually see from my peripheral vision she's sitting bolt upright now with her body locked tight. Continuing, I relate this story just for Joslyn's benefit. "Times were really tough on her. She came from impoverished beginnings. While her mother helped with the baby, she's a diabetic and was on disability so she was struggling herself. To help make ends meet for everyone, Bebe took odd jobs when she could. Because she was really good at computers, those jobs ended up being in the field of cybercrime."

Joslyn peeks at Bebe, and I spare her a glance. She's

glaring with her jaw locked tight, but I ignore it. "It was petty stuff at first, but she soon caught the attention of a black-hat hacker group that saw her potential. The money they paid her was good, and when it became too damn good, she dropped out of school, I'm guessing because she saw it as a way to give her son and mother a good life, despite the fact what she was doing was felonious."

Bebe shoots up from the table, her face flushed red with anger.

I merely say in a quiet voice, "Sit, Bebe. I promise this will be worth your time."

She doesn't do as I say. Instead, she lifts her chin defiantly. She doesn't move to the door and call for the guard, so I return to my conversation with Joslyn.

"About seven years ago, she got pinched by the FBI in a huge cyber-espionage sting. Luckily for our nation's security, Bebe was caught just before she could complete the download of our nuclear arms codes, which the group she was working for was poised to sell to the Chinese. There was no trial. Bebe refused to name others in the organization and pled guilty to the charges, earning her thirty-five years in prison."

Gasping, Joslyn snaps around to take in Bebe, a mixture of disdain and empathy on her face. Bebe sighs, collapsing into her chair and giving me an irritated look. "So what's your point?" she asks.

"I find it fascinating you could have given up every-one else in the organization for immunity, yet you took the fall instead. And you were nothing but their paid monkey—one who happened to be good with comput-ers. You weren't the person the government wanted. You could have testified for your government, put away a bunch of criminal masterminds who are a threat to our nation, and lived a fulfilling life with your son. But you didn't."

Bebe's teeth gnash and grind, a muscle ticking in the corner of her eye.

"Your son… he'd be what… nine years old now?" I ask.

She remains silent.

"Your mom is raising him in Ohio where you're from. They come out to visit you twice a year, which I know is a huge hardship on them financially."

To my surprise, Bebe's eyes water and her gaze drops to her lap.

"Leave her alone," Joslyn whispers fiercely. When I swing around in surprise, she glares.

But Bebe is right where I want her, and I'm not about to let up. I turn to the prisoner and ask, "Why, Bebe? Why did you let yourself get caught? Because you're good… probably the best at what you did, and you should have never gotten caught."

"You were protecting someone," Dr. Ellery says in a

voice filled with awe and understanding. Now she gets why I came here, and her soothing voice is full of empathy. "Your son, right?"

It's what I suspected all along because someone of Bebe's caliber doesn't get caught. Someone who's good enough to hack the NSA doesn't simply let themselves get caught, but Bebe did. And then she rolled over, pled guilty, and went to prison for a good chunk of her life without even a fight.

Bebe searches Dr. Ellery's face. For a moment, I can see something in Bebe's expression that might spell the need to release a pent-up secret. But then it's gone, and her eyes turn cold and silent.

I know deep in my gut Dr. Ellery has guessed what I've suspected, but I need Bebe to say it. To confirm my hunch about her before I go out on a limb to gain her freedom.

But she's not budging. After a long, hard look at me, she starts to stand from the chair and I'm immensely disappointed. She would have been such an asset to Jameson. More importantly, I need her on Joslyn's case.

Bebe is stopped, however, when Joslyn reaches a hand out and places it on Bebe's forearm. It's the lightest of touches, yet Bebe stops, twisting her neck to focus on her.

"You can trust Kynan," Joslyn says softly. "He's the real deal. I've put my life in his hands because I trust him, and I promise you… he can help you if you just tell him what he wants to know."

It's a sweet effort and I'm touched by the sincerity, but it doesn't appear to sway Bebe. She just stares at Joslyn, her lips pressed in a thin line of distrust. My mind moves to my backup plan, a man I heard about who works in the CIA in their cyber-espionage division. I can lure him away easily, but he's not as good as Bebe.

"His name is Aaron," Bebe says quietly as she sinks into her chair. She smiles at Joslyn, then addresses me. "My son's name is Aaron, and they threatened to kill him if I didn't get the codes for them."

"You were a mother first and a hacker second," Dr. Ellery says softly, an understanding smile on her face.

Bebe gives a nod but clarifies. "I was a mother first and a patriot second. I wasn't about to give away nuclear codes to anyone. So I left an obvious trail of crumbs as I hacked my way into the database, and I made sure I got caught."

Joslyn now is fully invested and asks her own questions. "But why not give up the people you worked for?"

"Because word was passed to me very quickly that they'd kill Aaron and my mom if I did."

"Oh, wow," Joslyn whispers, her eyes full of sorrow for Bebe.

"And so you gave up your life and your freedom to protect your son and your country." It's exactly as I suspected, but I had needed to know if I was right, and, more importantly, if she would be willing to put her trust in me to tell me. For all she knows, I could work for that black-hat group and I'm here to test her loyalty about keeping her mouth shut.

"I don't regret what I did," Bebe replies tersely.

"Why would you?" I ask with a smile. "It was the right thing to do."

I cock an eyebrow at Dr. Ellery. "Do I offer her the job?"

"Yes," she replies with a firm nod of her head. "I do believe you should."

The smile I bestow on Bebe is genuine. "How would you like to get out of prison today and come to work for me?"

CHAPTER 8

Joslyn

I STARE AT Kynan as he sits in the sleek, leather captain's chair on a private Leer jet after just having walked out of a federal maximum-security prison with one of the actual prisoners by his side.

My review of him is critical, searching for signs of some type of holiness because right now, I'm thinking he has some super powers I knew nothing about.

I mean... who in the hell has the ability to walk into a prison and come out with a prisoner?

"What's his deal?" the woman who is sitting beside me asks.

My neck twists slowly, and I tilt my head at Bebe Grimshaw. She hasn't said a word to me since the jet took off almost two and a half hours ago. We parted ways with Dr. Ellery, and she flew back to God knows where she was from. Kynan didn't bother saying, and I didn't ask.

I was afraid to ask him anything. Frankly, because I've so deified him since his miracle of springing Bebe from jail that I'm not sure I want to hear anything he has to say.

My gaze goes to Kynan, who is doing a good job ignoring us as he works on his laptop with headphones on.

"I have no clue," I drawl in confusion. "I mean... I thought I knew. He does security and protection work. I hired him to protect me."

"And yet, he has some pretty powerful connections," Bebe muses. "He had my release from prison already pre-arranged. That only comes from extremely high up in the government, and I'm sure it's off the books."

"I almost feel sorry for my stalker," I say in awe as I continue to stare at Kynan.

Bebe snorts. "What's the deal with this stalker of yours?"

That direct question snaps me out of my thrall, and I turn in my seat to face her. The jet we're on has four rows, two large captain's chairs on either side. The first two rows face the rear of the plane and the second face forward. It's how I'm able to stare at Kynan—in the first row—in miraculous wonder.

"A few years ago, someone started sending me creepy letters and gifts. When it escalated, I moved a few times trying to hide, but he always found me. Three days ago, he managed to break into my house and tried to strangle me, but the police got there before he could finish the job. I hired Kynan the next day."

Bebe's brow furrows. "No offense… but why would a man who has the power to spring a national security risk from prison help you? It's sort of small potatoes."

"No offense taken," I reply with a smile. "We have a history together."

Her face brightens in understanding. "I kind of got the sense something was there."

"Oh no," I insist, bringing both my hands up in denial. "Nothing there. We dated for about three seconds like twelve years ago."

Bebe purses her lips. "It's more than that."

And she's right. We had more than that. We were more than just a blip of time. But I don't want to say that out loud because over the years, I'd been able to minimize my heart break. Time does indeed dull the pain. While I've never let go of the truth that Kynan was most definitely the love of my life, I have been able to let go of the fact we missed our chance.

"Doesn't matter," I say dismissively. "It was a long time ago, but I'm very grateful he's taken my case."

"Just as I'm grateful he sprang me from prison," she murmurs thoughtfully.

"And gave you a job," I add. I had sat there quietly while Kynan offered her an incredible salary to be his own personal hacker—the white-hat variety, of course—back at the Jameson offices in Pittsburgh. This put her in close proximity to her son and mother. Kynan promised to help set them all up in a house together if she wanted that. Bebe, who seems like an incredibly tough woman to have survived in prison for seven years, had started weeping.

Kynan is bringing Bebe to California with us since he wants her to help set up a new security system at my house and do an audit of my own computer and internet system.

"I've got some clothes you can wear when we get to my house," I offer Bebe, and she blinks in surprise. "I think we're about the same size, although you're a few inches taller than me."

"That's not necessary," she grumbles, her face flushing as she glances at the khaki shirt and pants she'd been wearing when she left the prison. She also had a box with a few books, but it was mostly filled with letters and drawings from her son, Aaron.

"I don't mind," I assure her. "Lord knows I've got way too many clothes to begin with."

"That's nice of you," she mutters, ducking her head to stare out the window. Then she adds, "Thanks."

Smiling, I turn my attention to Kynan, only to find him watching me curiously. He still has his headphones on so he couldn't hear what we were just talking about. Not that it was a matter of national security.

Although if it was, I bet he'd already know about it.

Given his impressive connections and all.

◆

I WONDERED WHAT I'd be feeling when I pulled up to my house, having last left in a police car. They took me down to the precinct station about two miles from my house for a detailed interview. I refused medical attention, despite the fact I'd already had extreme bruising around my throat. I just wanted to get the interview done, so I could get to the airport and head to Vegas and Kynan.

As Kynan shuts off the rental car we'd picked up at the airport and I open the passenger door, Lynn comes out of my house. When I'd talked to her yesterday from Pittsburgh, she assured me she'd have the house ready for my arrival.

I knew what that meant. Not only would she have the place cleaned and the guest rooms freshened up with new sheets and towels, but she'd have all evidence of my attack erased. Broken glass from his entrance and black fingerprint dust would be eradicated so as not to distress me. Lynn was much more than a manager to me. She was my friend. She'd go above and beyond to make my homecoming as easy as possible.

Lynn comes off the porch and down the short, curved sidewalk that connects to the driveway. She's fifty-seven years old, rounder than she'd like, and wears her silvery-gray hair in a short cap. Her arms open, and I step into her embrace. "Glad to have you back, honey."

"Thanks for handling everything." I give her a hard squeeze before I pull away.

Turning to my new guests, I introduce my manager. "Lynn... this is Kynan McGrath and Bebe Grimshaw from Jameson Force Security."

If Lynn is flummoxed by Kynan's insanely gorgeous looks or by the fact Bebe is in a prison uniform, she doesn't show a hint of discord. She smiles, shakes hands, and then motions us into my home.

It's a shame, really. I had hoped this house was going to be my last purchase until I was perhaps ready to retire. It was my third move in two years, attempting to throw my stalker off my trail. I bought it under a blind trust so my name wouldn't be associated with it at all. I had my realtor sign a non-disclosure as well as the movers I'd hired. Even my utilities were under an alias.

And still... he found me.

"I took the liberty of ordering some food for all of you," Lynn says as she opens the front door and leads us in.

This place really was sort of my dream home. Just under five thousand square feet and a Santa Barbara zip code, it sits in a prime location with views of both the mountains and the ocean. It's bright and airy with wood beam ceilings, expansive windows, and French doors in every exterior room that leads to private balconies.

Oh, and it has a panic room, which was very appealing to me.

We follow Lynn into the French-country style kitchen I adore. She called my favorite catering company, and the counter is loaded with a variety of salads, grilled kabobs, fresh fruit, and mini key lime pies.

"Thank you so much, Lynn," I say as I walk over to a cupboard and pull out some plates. When I turn around, Kynan is letting his gaze roam around while Bebe has her hands clasped tightly in front of her, appearing incredibly awkward.

"What do you guys want to drink?" I ask as Lynn heads to the fridge. "I've got water, soda, beer, or wine."

"I'll take a soda," Bebe replies eagerly, and I wonder what it will taste like after seven years of prison food and drink.

"I'll be back," Kynan says. He disappears into the dining room, which leads into a formal living room.

I set the plates down, intent on following him, but Bebe shakes her head. "Let him check your place out. It's his job."

A bolt of fear hits me in the gut like a sucker punch. I almost double over as I realize... my stalker could actually be in my house right now. We all assumed he's off hiding and licking his wounds, but he's also bat-shit crazy so why wouldn't he be here, waiting for me to return?

"It's already been secured," Lynn says, and Bebe and I both turn to her. "Kynan had some of his folks from Vegas out here yesterday. They were updating the security system. A woman named Rachel is still here. Or rather, she's at her hotel right now. She'll be by later."

My jaw drops slightly, amazed by Kynan's foresight. But really, why should I be surprised? Of course he'd have had this place scoped out before he brought me here. This is the man who performs prison breaks with a wink of his eye.

He's Kynan McGrath, and he's going to be one step ahead of my stalker at all times.

I immediately experience that sensation of warmth and security again, trusting in the man who I hired to protect me. I'm safe here.

He'll protect me.

I have nothing at all to worry about.

CHAPTER 9

Kynan

HAVING GRABBED A bottle of beer out of the refrigerator, I make my way through to the back patio that's accessed from the formal living room. I'd patrolled the grounds earlier—almost a full two acres surrounded by a combination of fencing and hedges but still plenty of places to sneak in—and found them to be incredibly beautiful. The house has quieted as both Joslyn and Bebe made their way to their bedrooms about an hour ago. Most of the evening I'd spent with Bebe, getting her up and running on a brand-new laptop I'd had Rachel buy per Bebe's specifications.

I step out onto the patio, moving past a large wrought-iron table that seats six and overlooks the pool. Cutting to the right, I walk up five steps to a smaller patio that has a cement banister around the edge covered with flowering vines. From this vantage point, had the sun still been in the sky, I'd be able to clearly see the Pacific Ocean. As it is, I can barely see the moonlight glinting off the water but not much else. The rest of the valley is twinkling with lights.

Joslyn certainly has done well for herself, but I'm not surprised. From the first time I saw her on stage when she was just nineteen and bringing down the house in Vegas, I knew she was destined for big things.

Since we broke up, she's won multiple Grammys, filmed successful movies, and performed concerts in venues all over the world. She's an A-lister in Hollywood known for her triple threat of acting, singing, and dancing. Her last major success was a year on Broadway with a Tony award to prove her success there.

Yeah, I've followed her career and I've always wondered "what if". What if we'd stayed together? Would I have been traveling the world with her, riding on the coattails of her success? I feel safe in saying I wouldn't be doing what I'm doing these days had I gone with her. I would have let Joslyn have her chance to shine, and I would have been by her side for the long haul.

But that didn't fucking happen because for some unexplainable reason, she decided she wasn't in love with me and left without giving me a clear understanding of what was going through her head.

I was bitter for a long time.

Years, actually.

But then I moved past it.

Sort of.

I wouldn't let myself get trapped by a relationship

again, always reserving a healthy dose of skepticism over a woman's motives. Joslyn and her abrupt way of breaking things off made it incredibly easy to keep every other woman at arm's length. It was merely safer that way.

The last few years, I've rarely thought about her. When I would see something on TV or her name in the news, more often than not, I might even have a fond memory of her. Certainly, the bitterness had ebbed away like a low tide.

Which is why it bothers me that I'm so on edge around Joslyn now. There was initial anger she reached out to me, but damn if that didn't go ice cold when I found out she'd almost been killed by a stalker. Since then, I've been fueled by determination to keep her safe and hopefully have a bit of a face to face with this douchebag so I can make him regret putting his hands on her.

I try to focus on that. I really do. But when I'm in Joslyn's presence, it's difficult to think about anything other than how beautiful she is, or how soft I know her skin to be, or how amazing it was when I was fucking her.

Some would say it may have been the blush of my first and only real love, but it's not. Joslyn is just the best fuck I've ever had. Every single thing about her from the smell of her hair to the way her tongue would slide against mine, or even the taste of her pussy... there's never been better.

And goddamn it all to hell... I fucking want it again.

And badly.

It would be completely inappropriate for me to act on as she's my client and paying me good money to do a job for her—one that does not include sex and orgasms.

Besides that, Joslyn hasn't given one indication she thinks about me in the same way. She's not tried to flirt or dress provocatively—the sexy sleep outfit last night doesn't count as she wore it to bed without ever intending for me to see it—and she's been very much held in reserve around me.

For a man of thirty-eight years who has always been incredibly confident and sure of himself, the fact she's got my stomach all churned up is really pissing me off. I hope to fuck I can lure this maniac out quickly, dispatch the fucker, and get back on to my new life in Pittsburgh.

I crack my beer open and take a long pull, considering my game plan to lure Joslyn's stalker out into the open. It's ballsy and full of risk, but I believe we can pull it off. I don't see any other way unless Joslyn were just to go back about her life and wait for the guy to strike again. That's not even an option really. Who could live like that?

I know I sure as fuck couldn't.

The sounds of the French door opening behind me

causes me my spine to stiffen and I glance over my shoulder to see Joslyn walking out to join me. I knew it would be her. Sensed it. Felt the vibe. Prickled with awareness. Whatever the fuck it's called, I felt her coming before I saw her.

While the patio lights are off, there's enough landscape lighting around the hedges and in the bushes to easily see she's got a glass of wine in her hand as she walks my way. I bristle at the thought she'd want to join me out here for a relaxing drink because nothing about Joslyn inspires relaxation.

I don't say a word, though, as she comes up the steps and strides right up to the banister to stand beside me. She bends at the waist, puts her forearms on the cement top, and gazes out at the horizon silently.

"You should get some rest," I grumble before I take a sip of my beer. I move a step to the left to put some distance between us.

"I know," she replies quietly. "I tried, but I just can't. I usually come out here when I can't sleep. I didn't mean to disturb you."

"It's your house." My reply is curt and assholish. "Do what you want."

"I will," she snaps, showing a very brief glimpse of the sass I used to appreciate so much about this woman. But instead of turning me on, it pisses me off more, because that sass isn't being offered to amuse me.

It's not for my appreciation and respect.

It belongs only to her and never to me.

"You really should get your ass to bed, woman," I growl.

"Why are you being such a dick to me?" she demands. There's a landscape light just below her in the flowering vines, and her face is illuminated enough to see the flash of anger in her eyes. "I don't deserve it."

"You don't deserve it?" I sneer. Clearly, the bitterness I'd thought I'd let go of is sneaking back out. "You honestly don't think you deserve it?"

"No," she yells, her hand holding the wineglass shaking terribly in her fury. "I don't deserve it. I never did a thing to warrant this, and I have to wonder what happened in your life that turned you into such an asshole."

God, that makes me fucking laugh. Doubled at the waist, I laugh, incredulous she would ever think to point a finger. I straighten, lean toward her, and taunt, "You've got some fucking nerve, Joslyn. You leave me high and dry twelve years ago without a goddamn explanation... and you're curious as to why I'm being an asshole to you?"

Joslyn's eyes narrow and spark with fury. Leaning into me, she practically hisses, "You were fucking cheating on me, you sanctimonious prick. I didn't owe you anything except a goodbye."

I'm so stunned by her allegation I step backward as if she'd slapped me in the face. "Excuse me?"

"You heard me." She advances, pokes a delicate finger in my chest. "You were screwing someone else while you were proclaiming to love me. You were a cheating, dirty bastard, and you should count yourself lucky I gave you the courtesy of a goodbye."

My ears start buzzing, my blood boiling with rage. "You are bloody fucking mental. I never cheated on you."

"You did," she proclaims bitterly, tears welling in her eyes. "I saw the pictures."

"That's a fucking lie," I growl, a dangerous sound that should cause her to be cautious because I've had about enough of this shit.

She doesn't know me anymore, though, so she doesn't appreciate the peril she's in. A tear slips down her cheek, and she dashes it away. "My mom showed me a picture of you hugging another woman outside of her hotel room. And I saw the report from the investigator she hired. He had receipts and copies of text messages and emails between you and that woman."

"What?" I whisper, feeling my blood pressure climbing.

"My mom hired an investigator," she blabs, but I can only focus on one word.

Mom.

Her mom.

The woman who couldn't stand me and thought I was a distraction to her daughter.

"You were followed. Your phone was hacked, and there were messages and emails. I saw the printouts. There was a huge report. And like I said... I saw a photo of you hugging a woman outside—"

"Where is it?" I interrupt.

"What?"

My words come out harsh and clipped. "Where is the photo? The report? I know damn well you probably saved it all. After all, you put a lot of damn stock in something I was never shown so I could defend myself."

Joslyn opens her mouth, perhaps to deny, then snaps it shut just as fast. She pivots and stalks stiffly off the patio without a word. I follow behind her.

She leads me into the house, through the great room, and then to her study. It's the only room in her house I found to be messy and lived in. Scattered sheets of paper are all over her desk with song lyrics scribbled out in messy handwriting. Shelves stocked full of books— fiction and non-fiction alike. A stack of unread magazines on the floor. A heap of unread mail on the credenza behind her desk. A recipe book on the windowsill with yellow post-it notes flagging certain pages of interest.

Yeah... she spends a lot of time in here.

Joslyn sets her wine down on her desk before moving

to a set of built-ins. She pulls open a drawer that holds hanging files, then rifles through to one near the back. With an audible sigh, she pulls it free, turning to face me.

Slowly stretching an arm out, she hands me the file. I set my beer down, then take the folder from her.

It's blue with an expanding, reinforced spine, yet the contents inside are so thin they'd have fit in an envelope. I glance up to see Joslyn watching me with her arms crossed protectively around her midsection.

I open the file, letting my eyes fall to the documentation that caused this woman to drop me like a hot potato without an explanation.

On the top is a printed four-by-six photo, clearly taken at a distance as evidenced by the grainy resolution. But there I am, facing the camera and hugging a redhead in front of a hotel door. I instantly know who it is.

"That's Rachel," I say as I hold the photo out so it faces Joslyn. She jolts, her eyes widening with surprise. Leaning in, she stares hard at the picture. In disbelief, she murmurs, "No."

"Yes," I reply firmly. I easily recall back to twelve years ago when Joslyn and I were together. Jerico had just started up The Jameson Group. Rachel and I were just friends, and she had come to Vegas for a visit. I picked her up, and I took her to lunch.

We most certainly didn't fuck.

I toss the photo on Joslyn's desk and go through the folder in my hand. There's a document entitled *Investigative Report* by some hack detective agency—if the crummy quality of the letterhead is any indication. I skim the contents, note it's nothing more than typed entries by someone—dated and time stamped—indicating places I'd been with the pictured "woman," including times at my apartment as well as a hotel over a four-day period. Behind that, there's a list—again, just typed by this "investigator"—of made-up text messages and emails.

All lies.

I drop the folder on her desk with disgust. "I can't believe you fucking fell for that."

"Excuse me?" she replies defensively, her arms uncrossing and her hands going to her hips.

"That's all bullshit." I point to the folder. "Except the photo. That's legit. Rachel came to town and visited. We had lunch. We were going to go rock climbing one day, but I couldn't break away from work. Then she left. She wasn't working at Jameson then."

"I—I—" Joslyn stammers, but then grits her teeth. "The text messages and emails."

"Fake," I reply blandly.

"No." She shakes her head in adamant denial.

"You were fucking gamed, Joslyn. By your own goddamn mother."

"She wouldn't—"

"She fucking did," I snarl. But then I lose my shit, twelve years of hurt and frustration bubbling over. "And you were stupid enough to fucking fall for it. Christ, how could you have been so sodden stupid? How could you have just accepted that bloody crock of shit and not trusted in me, huh?"

"I didn't—"

I hold my hand up, cutting her words off. "But seriously... I was the stupid one for even falling for you in the first place."

Tears spring into her blue eyes. I whip away from the sight of them, stomping out of her office. God, I was a fucking fool and apparently still am, because even though I'm beyond pissed right now, my greatest instinct is to pull her into my arms and tell her all is forgiven.

But I don't because that's not who I am anymore.

I stalk through the entire house, making sure all doors are locked and secure. I double-check the alarm and make sure my gun is loaded. I don't expect any trouble tonight, but anything is possible. I'll be ready just in case.

CHAPTER 10

Joslyn

THE GLIDE OF something along my neck causes me to awaken. For a moment, I'm confused. I don't feel hands tightening around my throat, and I'm not being pinned down. Caught somewhere between a dream and reality, I feel the rough fingertips move to my jaw, which causes a tremor to shoot up my spine.

His voice feathers over me in a low whisper, recognizable and safe. "Shouldn't have shown me that file, Jos."

Not my stalker.

Kynan.

My eyes pop open. There's enough moonlight I can see him bending over me. His fingers grip my jaw, and his words are harsh, "I was better off not knowing the truth."

I bring my hand to his, not to try to pull away, but to press him to me. "I swear I didn't know that stuff was fake. You're right... I was so stupid."

"Not stupid," he chastises me gruffly. "Young and

easily misled."

"Why would she do that?" I cry out in frustration. "I hate—"

He responds by moving his hand to cover my mouth, cutting my rage against my mother off. "Don't want to talk about her."

I tilt my head, wondering if he can see the question in my eyes through the gloom of the night. Why wouldn't he want to talk about her? She screwed us both over. Took something that was magical and true, and ripped it all apart.

"Would rather see if you're wearing the same outfit you had on in Pittsburgh," Kynan murmurs, and it takes me a moment to process. His hand stays over my mouth, but the other moves to the sheet and comforter I'd pulled up to my shoulders.

The air hits my bare skin, but it's the knowledge he wants to see my body that has my nipples puckering tight. The blankets moving over them actually irritates— in the best of ways—and they're popping against the soft cotton of my camisole top. Not the same one as Pittsburgh, but similar. It's actually a nightie rather than a shirt and shorts set. My eyes have adjusted to the dark, and there's just enough moonlight to see Kynan watching the trail of the sheet as it reveals my body to him.

When I start to pant, Kynan twists to see me, his lips

set in a hard line. "Going to fuck you tonight, Jos. And don't even think to deny me the pleasure."

My breath comes out in a heavy rush through my nose, and Kynan slides his hand free from my mouth. He leans over, his lips hovering just over mine as he warns me, "In fact, your next words had better be 'Kiss me, Kynan' or there's going to be hell to pay."

I can't help it. A strange giggle of relief and yearning bubbles out of me, and I'm smiling when I say, "Kiss me, Kynan."

His teeth flash white, his eyes feral and hot. I expect his mouth to crash down on mine. Instead, it goes to my neck where his teeth graze over my skin.

Immediately, I know things are different. Twelve years ago… just a mere nineteen years old…I really didn't know much about sex. Kynan was only my second, and he taught me so much. But he was sweet and gentle with me, patiently guiding and urging and whispering lovely words.

I know instantly the Kynan McGrath *I'd* known is gone. That whatever has happened to him in the last twelve years has changed him. He is not a sweet and gentle lover anymore. That knowledge excites me like nothing ever has, and I can feel wetness seeping into my panties.

Kynan scrapes his teeth along my throat, all the way to the center of my chest where he presses a kiss. His hands press into the mattress by my ribs, then he's biting my nipple through my cotton nightie.

Crying out, I clamp my hands onto his head—not to push him away, but to pull him tighter. Definitely tighter. He sucks hard, wetting the hard nub through the fabric and causing my hips to buck upward.

I try to pull him up, make him kiss me on the mouth, but then his body is on top of mine. Heavy and safe. My legs part, wanting him to settle his hard, thick length right up against my core.

Kynan tugs at my nipple with his teeth one more time before he presses his face into my belly. My hands are still at the sides of his head, and I drive my fingers into his thick hair. He inhales so sharply I know he's seeking something past the scent of my fabric softener. A low growl rumbles from deep within him before he slides lower down my body.

My legs spread further.

He pushes my nightie up and then his mouth is at my core, hot breath seeping in through my silk panties.

I bolt upright, my hands once again finding his head, which he lifts ever so slightly. We stare at each other through the dark, but there's enough moonlight hitting his brown eyes to recognize the desire sizzling there.

"Tell me to kiss you again," he orders gruffly.

It's an effort to breathe, and my chest heaves under the pressure of it all. My entire body is trembling and tight all at the same time, and I feel like I might splinter from the slightest touch from Kynan.

Still, I take the risk and murmur, "Kiss me."

It's not my mouth I expect his lips to find, and he doesn't disappoint. His fingers are between my legs, sliding into my panties and pulling the crotch to the side. Lowering his head, Kynan finally gives me my kiss, and it's hot and wet as he covers me.

I can't control the long groan of relief from the attention of his mouth and tongue between my legs. He attacks me ferociously, and it's obvious he's seeking one thing and one thing only.

For me to come for him hard and fast.

It happens mere moments after he presses a long finger inside of me while sucking on my clit. My back arches deeply off the bed as a powerful orgasm sweeps through me. It's so intense my mind actually goes blissfully blank for a moment, and all I can do is tumble along with the sensations racking my body.

I'm floating, light as a feather and barely aware, as my panties are stripped down my legs. Of Kynan going to his knees so he can work at his belt. Once he slides it off, I blink slowly while watching him undo his jeans. He reaches inside, then take himself in hand.

I'm still floating on the minor tremors of the previous orgasm as he strokes himself a few times.

Kynan covers me, putting an elbow to the mattress,

and I raise my legs. Then he's thick and hot, pressing inside of me. I glide my hands into the back of his opened jeans, grasp at the hard muscles of his ass, and try to pull him inside of me.

He slides in inch by glorious inch.

Stretching me. Filling me so deeply.

Kynan groans when he bottoms out, bending his neck so our foreheads touch ever so slightly. His breath flutters over my face before his lips finally find mine.

A sigh of happiness floats from my mouth to his, and he starts to move. Kynan kisses me deeply as his hips drive into me. I remember this feeling... of being with him—him inside of me—and it's one of pure completeness. I've never felt it since in the relationships I've had, and I'm surprised I feel it now given the time and distance between us.

For so long, I hadn't thought I was good enough for him. I thought he'd lied to me when he said he loved me. I'd felt a million times the fool over falling for him.

But that's all gone now. Every bit of the anger and betrayal had disappeared. I don't know if he feels it, but the connection I feel to him right now is far beyond just the way our bodies are joined.

I can feel my body quickening again, then tightening. When I groan into Kynan's mouth, he pumps into me harder. Lifting his head slightly, he takes me in. I try to read something in his eyes, but they're completely glazed with lust and primal need.

My second orgasm hits me by surprise. I call out his name when it does, bucking under him.

"Christ," Kynan groans as he pounds into me. Suddenly, he goes still, his face moving to press into my neck and his arms banding tightly around me. His hips buck hard one more time, sending his cock into me deeper than ever, and I know he's coming. It's done silently, but I yearn to hear my name from his lips.

But I only get a groan of relief as his body shudders slightly while he unloads.

We're both still for a few moments. I let my fingers drift over his lower back in a soft caress. Sighing against my neck, Kynan lifts his head.

He gazes at me, a contemplative look I think might spell the beginning of a deep conversation. God, do we have stuff to talk about.

But then he's gone.

Slipping easily out of me. Rolling right off me.

Walking right out of my room as he zips up his pants, and he's just... gone.

CHAPTER 11

Kynan

I POUR ANOTHER cup of coffee, glancing at the digital clock above the double oven unit. Joslyn's manager, Lynn, and her publicist, Harry Hnatkovich, should be here soon.

Bebe is tapping away on her laptop, checking the security cameras I'd ordered to be installed around the property. Rachel had flown down here to work on securing Joslyn's home while I'd gone to Pittsburgh to interview Cruce. I'd had her upgrade the alarm system, put in high-tech, ultra-resolution cameras with motion-sensor spotlights, and do a sweep of the entire house to ensure it had not been bugged somehow by the stalker. It thankfully came out clean.

Rachel holds out her cup as she watches over Bebe's shoulder, a silent plea for a refill. I cap her off, glancing through the kitchen to the great room and the hall beyond that leads to the master suite. I expect Joslyn to come wandering out at any moment. She knows our meeting with Lynn and Harry is set to start at nine, and I expect her to show long before that. Joslyn's always been an early riser.

But let's face it... I'm sure she's doing her best to avoid me after last night. I pulled the ultimate dick move—one of the worst a man can do to a woman—and that was leaving her bed without any post-fucking cuddles or explanation for the abrupt end to the evening.

It was hard disentangling myself from Joslyn, our relationship having become suddenly complicated beyond understanding. Within a matter of moments, everything I thought I'd known about her changed. When she showed me the folder her mom had deceitfully put together, I was faced with the realization my life had been manipulated and something had been taken away from me. My anger was mainly for Madeline Meyers, the mastermind who'd succeeded in tearing Joslyn and me apart.

That initial anger subsided enough to drive me to do something stupid. After stewing in anger, regret, and twelve years of not having the best fucking sex of my life, I'd reasoned I could have it again. It was there for the taking, and I was sure Joslyn would feel the same. She'd been cheated as severely as I had.

At face value, it was a good plan. Joslyn had opened her arms and spread her legs willingly for me. It was like a homecoming when I sank inside her, and I had the best bloody orgasm of my entire life.

Hands down... the absolute fucking best.

So goddamn good that when the last tremor faded away, I immediately got angry I'd been denied her for twelve years. Madeline wasn't here for me to take my anger out on, but Joslyn was. As she'd gazed up with soft eyes, her pussy still clenching hard around my spent cock, it had pissed me off because part of it was on her, too. Joslyn should have questioned that shit. She should have given me the benefit of the doubt, and she should have pushed back at her mother to see the truth. At the very bloody least, she should have fucking showed me the folder twelve years ago so I would have had a chance to defend myself.

Yeah... it pissed me off so bad I'd had to get away from Joslyn. So I left her without a word, returned to my room, and grabbed my gun. I stayed up most of the night. Sitting out on the couch, I'd hoped that fuckwad of a stalker had the balls to try to come after her, which would give me a chance to blow him away.

Sadly, that hadn't happened.

"...copies of the letters and I'll get them analyzed, but Kitchner doesn't put any stock into this being a serial type thing."

Blinking, I try to focus on Rachel. "I'm sorry... what?"

She rolls her eyes, and she's the only employee I'd let get away with doing that. "You clearly weren't listening to me. I was telling you that I met with Detective Kitchner yesterday. He let me go through the evidence they've collected, which is pitifully little. Mostly just the gifts he'd left Joslyn, which included one eviscerated cat he'd hung on her gate and they have in freezer storage."

"And you said he doesn't think this guy has done it before?" I prompt, proving I was listening... somewhat. "Why not?"

Rachel shrugs. "The detective thinks when the stalker told Joslyn that she was his favorite, it was just taunting."

"And this detective bases that on what?"

She shrugs again. "I got the distinct impression he had bigger fish to fry. Given the lack of any fingerprints or DNA left behind, I doubt he's going to put much work into this situation right now."

"Typical," I growl, then take a sip of coffee. Just as I'm lowering the mug, I see Joslyn over the rim.

Her hair is wet, face scrubbed of makeup, and there are dark circles under her eyes. She apparently got as little sleep as I had.

Wearing a pair of gray leggings and an off-the-shoulder white t-shirt, she's easily the most beautiful thing I've ever beheld. Barely looks a day older than nineteen.

Her eyes hold mine as she steps into the kitchen, and there's definitely an awkward tension. I try to break the ice by updating her on what Rachel had found out from

Kitchner.

"Without any fingerprints or DNA to go on right now, we've got barely anything to help us identify this guy."

Joslyn doesn't flinch or give anything away in her expression. She rounds the island and comes toward me. I'm presuming for a cup of coffee.

"But that's all moot." I mean for it to be reassuring—a testament to the fact I intend to lure this asshole right into a trap.

Joslyn merely continues until she's right in front of me, then cocks her hand back and slaps me across the face. It's hard enough to force my head to snap sideways.

"Oh, damn," Rachel murmurs. A brief glance at Bebe shows she's frozen, gaping from behind her laptop.

I settle my astonished attention on Joslyn. Her eyes are flaming with indignation as she mutters, "You're an asshole, Kynan McGrath. In the future, do your job and keep your hands to yourself. You do that, and we're good. Got me?"

The flush of anger and embarrassment layer on top of the heated imprint her hand left behind, but I merely nod as I grit out, "I got you."

"Good," she says with an icy smile before turning to her cabinet for a coffee mug.

Rachel raises an eyebrow, but I just shrug. Bebe returns to furiously typing on her keyboard.

The doorbell rings, and Joslyn puts her cup down. "That will be Lynn and Harry. I'll go let them in."

I grab the coffee pot, lean over, and fill her cup, pointedly ignoring Rachel, whose eyes I can still feel on me. I'm sure wanting to know why in the hell our client just slapped me. Ordinarily, as an employer, I'd worry about it, but Rachel knows my history with Joslyn.

I'm saved from having to meet her gaze by Joslyn returning to the kitchen with Lynn and a smartly dressed man who appears to be in his early thirties.

There are no introductions made. The man is carrying a large vase of fresh flowers—sunflowers to be exact—which are Joslyn's favorites. It's strange, the trivial things we remember from years ago.

For a moment, I have a flash of jealousy over her publicist bringing her flowers. She didn't indicate they were in a relationship, but then I notice how pale Joslyn is.

When Harry sets the vase on the counter, I survey the sunflowers. "These were sitting at the edge of the front yard that borders the neighbor. I thought it was odd they were just sitting there, so I stopped to examine them more closely."

Lynn's hand flutters near her throat. "They're from *him*."

Reaching out, I snatch the plain white card that's stuck in a plastic holder with no envelope. It doesn't identify a flower shop, and it only has two simple words. *Welcome home.*

"Maybe they're not meant for Joslyn," Harry says hesitantly. It's evident by his voice he really, really wants to believe that.

But I know they're meant for Joslyn. We all do.

Turning to Bebe, I order, "Pull up the camera feed for that quadrant."

"Already on it," she says from a position hunched over her keyboard. I walk around the island to come up behind her. Rachel, Joslyn, Lynn, and Harry all do the same.

Bebe pulls up the footage, then starts a visual rewind. I watch the clock move backward in fast motion, catching the occasional stray car driving by.

"There," Rachel exclaims. Bebe stops the rewind, playing the footage. We all lean forward and watch.

Just on the very outside edge of the screen, a hooded figure appears. The motion trips the camera's spotlight to come on, illuminating the figure.

He's carrying the vase of sunflowers, then sets them carefully on the grass before turning away and disappearing off the screen.

"Play it again," I demand.

She does... three more times.

"How do we know that's him?" Harry asks, the first to break the silence. Joslyn moves over to the island, then picks up her coffee cup. Lynn goes to the cabinet to get a mug for herself.

"It's him," Rachel says assuredly.

"It's absolutely him," I say in agreement. "The way he dressed in a hoodie pulled up, he didn't want to be identified. He kept his shoulder turned so his face was never on camera. He also wasn't surprised by the light coming on when the camera did. Based on the fact he barely came into the view of the camera, it tells me he knew exactly where the camera was placed and what it could see."

"Which means he's been watching the house and is well aware of our new security updates," Rachel adds.

"I think you should move again," Lynn blurts out as she pours coffee. "At the very least, check into a hotel."

Rachel shakes her head. "No, this is good. This means he's still fixated on her. She's hardly been home a day, and he's already reached out. If she goes into hiding, we lose our chance to catch him."

"He's watching," I tell Lynn. "That means he'll be easy to lure into the open."

Joslyn doesn't say a word. Leaning against the counter, she just sips her coffee.

I turn to Harry. "That's where we need you. Joslyn and I have to go public with our relationship."

"Relationship?" he asks in confusion.

"Fake relationship," I amend. "Figure out the best

way to get the news out to the biggest population of people."

"Cara Peterson," Harry says, and Lynn nods in agreement.

"Who is that?"

"Only the biggest talk show on TV these days," Lynn explains.

"That will work," I reply with a curt smile. Joslyn seems to be disconnected from all of this—stuck in her own head.

I leave it alone for now, addressing her manager and publicist. "For the next few weeks, book us in high-profile restaurants with paparazzi, secure tickets to shows, whatever it is you do to get your girl out there. I'll be by her side the entire time, hopefully pissing this guy off."

"We'll do an official press release," Harry says as he whips out his phone and starts typing notes into it. "I can get her on Cara's show pretty easy. She owes me a favor."

"I don't like this," Lynn reiterates, pointedly gesturing at Joslyn, who has her gaze pinned on her coffee cup. Lynn puts her arm on Joslyn's shoulder, and she reluctantly turns to her manager. "I think this is just too dangerous."

"She'll never be by herself," I reassure her, and Lynn swings my way, eyes heavy with distrust. "I promise she will be protected at all times."

Giving my attention to Joslyn, I address her specifically. "But you have to be okay with this, Jos."

She finally acknowledges me, the first time since she slapped my face, which I admittedly deserved. Her look is fierce, not in anger but in determination to get this solved.

She then turns to Lynn, taking her hand. "I trust Kynan to protect me. I want to do this. If we don't do something affirmative, it could be weeks or months where I'm living in fear. I want to be able to move on with my life and put all of this behind me."

Her words are simple, easily explaining where her head must be these days with having a stalker come after her. But I can't help but feel those words are also specifically directed at me. That she wants to move past me, what we had, and what we did last night, ending with me giving her a metaphorical slap in the face by leaving her without talking.

Yeah, I totally deserved that actual slap.

"Fine," Lynn says in capitulation, but then she pivots and points a finger directly at me. "But if Joslyn gets hurt, I'm going to cut your balls off."

"She'll be safe, I promise."

Lynn nods and turns to Joslyn. They huddle with Harry, starting to make plans to out us to Hollywood as a couple.

Rachel leans in toward me to murmur. "You've got

some explaining to do."

"Not to you," I answer, although I'll probably tell her at some point about what happened last night. Rachel is the least judgmental person I know. But for now, we have work to do. "I need you to get on all the local flower shops to see if you can find out who bought those flowers."

"That's a needle in a haystack," Rachel points out. "He could have bought those flowers four towns away."

"I know," I say with a wry smile. "But try, okay?"

"Of course," Rachel says, then asks Bebe. "Can you print me a list of all flower shops in a twenty-mile radius? I'll start with that."

"Sure," Bebe says as she starts tapping away at the keys. "But I can do you one better."

"How's that?" Rachel asks.

"I can try to hack into their systems to check their electronic records. It will take time, but at least it's something."

"You are brilliant." Rachel beams at Bebe, who flushes under the praise but turns worried eyes to me.

"That is..." she says. "If you want me to do that. It's not legal."

"Go for it." I'm not worried in the least. It's for a good reason, and it's not going to hurt the flower shop owners.

Bebe nods and gets to work, and I realize... if she has

luck with locating the guy this way, this could be over with very, very quickly.

I had sort of set my expectations this could take weeks to resolve—certainly several days at the least. But if Bebe is as good as I think she is, and this stalker was stupid enough to leave a trail, then my time with Joslyn is quickly ticking away.

I have no clue how that even makes me feel.

CHAPTER 12

Joslyn

AFTER I PULL another armful of hangers with clothing attached from my closet, I throw it on my bed. Picking up the one on top, I examine it. It's a silver Givenchy gown I'd worn to the Golden Globes five years ago, and I haven't worn it since. It's not proper in Hollywood to wear the same designer gown twice, so it just sits in my closet and collects dust.

With a quick critical eye, I determine it's not something Bebe could utilize until she can buy some clothes of her own.

Not that I expected to find anything in here she'd appreciate. I'd already raided my drawers yesterday not long after we'd arrived at my house. I know Bebe had to be dying to get rid of that prison uniform, so I'd gathered a bunch of casual stuff—shorts, t-shirts, jeans, and sweatpants. I'd even had a bunch of brand-new lingerie I'd never worn, although my bra size is about two cups too big for Bebe, I'm sure she was thankful for the fresh panties. I set her up right away in one of the guest rooms that has its own master bath so she could shower the stink of captivity off and start fresh.

Tossing the Givenchy gown to the left of the pile, I pick up the next item. An Oscar de la Renta black crepe pantsuit I'd not even worn yet. It still had the price tag on it, but it also went into the pile on the left. I'd donate it somewhere, although I have no clue who would actually wear this stuff. Or maybe I can have Harry auction it off and give the proceeds to charity.

"Spring cleaning?" I hear from my bedroom doorway, and I whip around to find Rachel standing there. "Can I come in?"

"Sure," I murmur, nabbing a flowery Gaultier above-the-knee dress I'd worn to some award luncheon. I'd managed to land a plum role in an indie film about a singer disillusioned with the business who gave it all up to start a new life in another country. Of course, she meets a handsome, mysterious man there and falls in love. The role hit close to home because I sometimes find myself so tired of everything that I wonder how bad it would be to walk away from it all.

I have to admit cutting out crazy stalkers from my life has great appeal.

Holding the dress up, I remember how great it looks on me. I love this freaking dress. I'd totally wear it again, be damned what the critics say. It starts a new pile to the right.

Rachel comes into my room, then plops down on the other side of my bed from the pile of clothing. She reclines on her side, propping her head in her hand and watching me.

I go through a few more outfits, all ending up in the auction pile. The silence isn't awkward, but it's not necessarily comfortable either. Just before I can start blabbering just to fill the void, Rachel says, "Lynn and Harry seem really nice."

"They're the best," I agree, shooting her a brief smile.

"And I think Bebe is going to be a game changer for us."

"Mmm, hmm."

"We'll have this asshole caught in no time," she says cheerfully.

"Counting on it." I put a Zac Posen skirt in the auction pile, but then reconsider, moving it to the small pile I'm keeping.

"Why did you slap Kynan?" Rachel asks, and my eyes snap to her in surprise. She merely smiles blandly. "I mean... I'm sure he deserved it because he wasn't mad about it."

My tongue feels glued to the top of my mouth. Being confronted about this out of the blue by a woman I don't know much about has me at a loss.

"You don't have to tell me," she continues. "But I figure it might be good for you to have someone to talk to. Clearly, something is going on between you two."

I deflate immediately, giving up the pretense I can just move on from what happened last night. I've not been able to think about anything else. How wonderful it was. How I felt such an intense connection with him.

How I'd—for the first time in as long as I can remember—felt hopeful about things.

Until he walked out of the room… and sent me crashing back down to earth with no soft landing in sight.

"He seduced me last night," I confess as I slowly raise my head to meet her eyes. She doesn't seem surprised. "I mean, came right into my room and started… well, he didn't give me much of a warning or room to say no."

"Be honest," Rachel chides. "You didn't want to say no."

The corners of my mouth pull upward, and I shake my head. "No. I didn't want to say no."

"Y'all had some serious issues," Rachel points out as she pushes up and maneuvers to sit Indian-style facing me. "How did you get past them?"

I give a mirthless laugh as I finger the next outfit on top of the waning pile in the middle. "I had thought he cheated on me, which is why I broke things off. Found out my mother had scammed me. Doctored up a fake report from an investigator. Threw in a picture of him hugging you."

"Me?" she asks in surprise.

"You came to visit him in Vegas around the time we were dating," I answer. "My mom did have someone following Kynan, and he snapped a picture of you two hugging. Coupled with some fake texts, emails, and receipts, it looked like he was two-timing me."

"Oh, wow," she murmurs as her gaze drifts to the pile of clothes before popping back up to me. "I bet Kynan was pissed."

I nod, my own anger building again. "Pissed enough to fuck me, make me think we had a connection, and then walk away without another word. He didn't even bother to get naked. Just unzipped his pants and—"

Rachel defensively holds up her hands. "TMI, Joslyn. TMI."

I take a deep breath, then let it out slowly. "The point being... I thought it meant something, but it clearly didn't to him. And truth be told... I think he acted that way to punish me for being so stupid all those years ago and falling for my mother's shit."

Empathy fills Rachel's eyes. "Maybe. But we all do stuff out of anger we regret later, and I know Kynan... he's not an inherently unkind man. He is an emotional one, though, and I'm betting he's having some regrets today."

I snort in disregard of such an assertion. I don't want to give him the benefit of the doubt on this, which is exactly what I was guilty of doing twelve years ago. The irony of that is obvious, but I don't give my body away easily. I have to feel something deep for a man. It hurt to know I was feeling it last night, while he was just feeling a good orgasm.

Or hell... maybe it wasn't even good for him.

"Ugh," I moan, snagging another outfit from the middle pile. I move to the free-standing full-length mirror in the corner of my room, then hold the red silk dress up in front of me. I'd worn it to the recording wrap party after my last album.

"Let's go shooting," Rachel suggests.

My brows draw together as I consider her through the mirror's reflection. "Shooting?"

"Guns," she replies smoothly. She swings her legs over the side of the bed where she bounds off. "It will be fun. You can imagine Kynan's face in the center of the target. Besides... you should know how to shoot a gun for protection."

"I know how to shoot a gun for protection," I mutter as I examine the dress. "I'm from Montana for God's sake."

"Then let's go shooting." Rachel grins like this is the best idea in the entire world. It's not, of course, but it is a lot better than cleaning out my closet.

"Okay," I finally manage to say, tossing the red dress on the bed and feeling a bit... lighter. Maybe aiming at an imaginary target of Kynan's head will improve my mood even more.

Rachel exits my room and I follow, nabbing my cell phone and purse from my dresser on the way out. When we make our way into the kitchen, I come up a bit short when I spot Kynan leaning on the kitchen island beside Bebe as she works on her laptop. He lifts his head, eyes locking on mine, and I can't read a damn thing on his expression. No remorse or regret. No triumph he got laid last night without much fuss.

"I'm taking Joslyn to a shooting range," Rachel announces as we step into the kitchen.

"No, you're not," Kynan replies with a nod to Bebe. "She's found a flower shop about five miles from here that had a large purchase of sunflowers yesterday. Customer paid cash, but they entered it into their system, which auto adjusts their stock requirements based on daily purchases. I need you to go there and interview the people who were on duty. See if you can get an ID on the guy."

"And also ask to see their security footage. They have cameras set up, but I didn't hack them. Don't want to draw unnecessary attention if we don't have to."

Rachel goes into full-on work mode, spine snapping straight. She gives me a short glance. "Sorry, Joslyn. Another time, okay?"

"Yeah, sure," I hasten to reassure her. "This is far

more important. But… I can go with you."

"You stay with me," Kynan growls, not even bothering to glance my way as he issues the order. His high-handedness grates on my nerves, but I realize deep down he's only doing it for my own protection and not to annoy me.

Rachel reaches out, touching my arm. She gestures toward the front door. "Walk me out, okay?"

"Sure," I reply softly and trail her out of the kitchen, through the great room, and to the large foyer to the double front doors. She picks up her rental car keys and backpack she'd left on a table before giving me her attention. "Listen… about what your mom did to you…"

I blink in surprise. "Yeah?"

"Don't leave that unresolved, okay?" she advises. "Call her, send her an email… whatever you feel is the best way to communicate with her, but let her know you know what she did and give her the opportunity to apologize for it."

"My mom doesn't apologize for anything," I mutter.

"Then at least you know she doesn't have any remorse and you can move on. But that was a huge betrayal to you, and that shit will only fester. Trust me, I know a little bit about this sort of stuff."

This takes me aback because while there's been plenty of anger inside of me toward my mom, I have not once considered confronting her about it. There didn't seem to be any purpose to it since we didn't have the greatest relationship anyway. She was so angry with me for firing her as my manager that she had no qualms with essentially cutting me out of her life for a few years. It wasn't until she remarried and her new husband urged her to reach out that we reconciled somewhat. I have to admit it hurt in those years we weren't talking, but I'd also learned to live with it.

I'd learned how to be alone and to depend only on myself, and I could certainly do that again. In fact, after I get this stuff resolved with my stalker, I am going to do a serious reevaluation of my life and what I really want out of it. I'm also going to genuinely consider what I want out of my career. After twelve plus years in the business, I'm getting worn out from the constant drain on my creative energies.

Maybe Rachel is right. Maybe that's something I should resolve sooner rather than later so I can have a clean slate when it comes time to reevaluate my life goals and priorities. Having that hanging over my head can't be good for my soul. Besides that, we have worked hard the last few years to put our relationship back in order.

I smile. "I'll do that. And thanks for the talk."

"Anytime," she says, then leans in and gives me an impulsive hug. I give her a return squeeze.

After she leaves, I lock the door and reset the alarm,

which Kynan has pounded into me must be set at all times whether I'm here or not.

I edge back into the kitchen. Kynan doesn't bother looking up, although I know he's heard me come in.

"I need to take a trip," I say, but he still doesn't give me his attention. He merely replies, "Give me about half an hour to finish some stuff up here with Bebe, then I'll take you wherever you want to go."

"Sounds good," I reply breezily as I head toward my room. Keeping my voice light, I nonchalantly offer over my shoulder, "We're heading to Cunningham Falls. I need to see my mother."

I don't wait for his response, catching only the briefest glance of his head popping up and his face flooding with shock.

I brace for him to argue it's not prudent or a valuable use of our time, but he doesn't. That satisfies me, and I start calculating whether I'll need an overnight bag. It's roughly a two-and-a-half-hour direct flight via private jet to Cunningham Falls from Santa Barbara. I've made the trip several times in the last few years. I decide our talk shouldn't take that long and I'd rather be back in my own bed tonight, so I have nothing really to put together. I'll freshen up my makeup, make a smoothie, and then hangout until Kynan is ready to leave.

CHAPTER 13

Kynan

THIS ISN'T MY first trip to Cunningham Falls, Montana, but it's been a long damn time. Jameson had been hired by Joslyn's mother to provide protective services for her. Joslyn was headlining a major casino in Vegas at the time. While she probably wasn't under any direct threat by fans, it made her mother feel better for Joslyn to have security guards. Plus, she'd negotiated it into the contract for the casino to pay for our services.

I'm not quite sure when I fell in love with Joslyn, but our fate was sealed by the end of the trip to Cunningham Falls. She'd come to give a charity benefit concert, the proceeds of which were going to a hospital wing named after her late father. Madeline had not wanted her to do the trip, but Joslyn had held firm in her resolve. I think it might have been the first time she'd actually stood up to her mother, a sure sign she was going to try to keep some control over her career. Perhaps that had actually been the beginning of their business relationship foundation cracking.

Regardless, we were here for two nights. It was on the second I gave into my desires and made love to Joslyn. We'd both fallen for each other fast in the few weeks I'd been assigned to protect her. We had hours during the day where it was just me and her, and it's surprising how fast people can grow to like each other when they have nothing to do but talk. Of course, the attraction was through the roof. It only took me kissing her in her hotel room in Cunningham Falls that night after the concert to know I could probably never stop kissing her.

We'd been stupid fucking kids. Just a few weeks later, her mom had shown Joslyn the doctored reports to make it appear as if I'd cheated. Let's face it... she didn't know me well enough to trust in me.

I drive the rental car through the sleepy town of Cunningham Falls. It's nearing four, and the sun is starting to hang low in the sky. It throws a beautiful shade of orange and pink over the snow-covered mountains, and I have to admit... this is one of the prettiest places I've ever been to in my life.

Joslyn hadn't called her mom, so this is going to be a surprise visit. I'm also using this trip as a way to test the stalker. I had Joslyn schedule the private jet by using her phone and credit card rather than Jameson resources as I'd been doing, which I would bill to Joslyn later. I wanted to lay some easy breadcrumbs to see if the stalker was on the same hacking level as Bebe. She laid down some triggers on the credit card company to see if an outside source pings her information. I'm doubting this guy is that sophisticated, but there's no telling.

I follow Joslyn's directions out of town to Madeline's new home. Other than conveying short and succinct sentences to me, obviously still more than a little annoyed with my behavior last night, Joslyn hasn't been much of a conversationalist. I did learn Madeline had married a man named Darren Dawes, who is a successful cattle and sheep rancher. I couldn't tell, though, whether Joslyn actually likes the guy as she's not in a sharing mood.

In Montana, it's possible to go miles and miles without seeing a house. There is no walking across the street to borrow a cup of sugar outside the city limits. We eventually come to a turn-off from the highway with a wooden arch held up by rough lumber posts that spell out—*Double-D Ranch*.

"Does your stepfather realize he named his ranch after a bra size?" I ask as I turn onto the dirt and gravel road.

I don't get a smile, a snort, or a snicker. Just a bland, "I'm sure he's been told that before."

Yup. She's still pissed, and I can't blame her. I deserved the slap, and I deserve her enmity. I'm going to let her hold onto it for just a bit, but then I'm going to resolve that shit. We were both riding high on emotion, but we have something between us that needs to be evaluated.

We come around a wide curve, then cross a small covered bridge that spans a gurgling creek before the ranch comes into view. I'd checked Darren Dawes out on the plane, and he makes some serious bank. The ranch house is actually fairly modest, though. I'd guess maybe about twenty-five-hundred square feet and sprawling since it's single story, and it's probably more than enough for him and Madeline. I'd learned he's about twenty years her senior and all his kids live outside of Montana.

There's a Mercedes coupe in the driveway that's probably a good five or so years old and a truck of about the same age. Off to the side, several more vehicles— ranch hands, I'd assume—near a two-story workshop. Beyond that, there are multiple barns and a silo. In the distance, snow-covered hills and a large butte, with lots of cattle in the immediate valley.

I pull up behind the Mercedes, then kill the engine. Joslyn lets out a pent-up breath, and I turn to face her. "You ready?"

She looks at me reluctantly. "As ready as I'll ever be."

"Want me to stay here?"

Joslyn shakes her head. "I sort of want the shock value of you being at my side. She has no clue I hired you a few days ago."

"Does she know about your stalker?" I ask.

Another shake of her head, her blond waves shimmering from the movement. "I didn't want to worry her."

No matter what Madeline has done to her daughter in the past, she still loves her mother very much. I hope this is something they can resolve.

Reaching over, I curl my hand around the back of her neck. The first time we've touched since I slid my cock out of her last night—not counting the face slap. She stiffens warily. "I'm glad you're doing this. It's a good idea, and I'll be right by you. You've got this."

Her slender throat moves as she swallows against what I'm betting is emotion and confusion from my supportive words. It's obvious she wants to hate me, but fuck if I'm going to let that happen. I know one thing after last night... I'm determined to see if there's something between us still.

"Thanks," she murmurs before pulling away from me. I let her go, although I could easily make her stay. I could hold her tight and we could talk this bloody nonsense out between us, but it's really not the time.

We exit the vehicle, and I don't bother locking it. I follow Joslyn up the wide porch steps and she gives a sturdy knock on the door. There's a dog yapping inside—small by the sound of it—and a woman's voice I immediately recognize as Madeline's calls out, "I'm coming."

The door swings open. Madeline Meyers—now Dawes—is standing there holding a furry white dog that's wiggling with excitement to have visitors in one arm. She's changed a lot in twelve years. Added a few pounds that actually look exceptionally good on her. She was always too fucking skinny I thought. The designer clothes are also gone, and she appears incredibly comfortable in a pair of jeans and a flannel shirt.

Her eyes land on Joslyn, and she shrieks with joy. "Joslyn... oh my word... what are you doing here?"

I'm standing behind Joslyn so I can't quite see her face, but if the ice in her tone is any indication, there's no warm smile being given in return. "Sorry for the intrusion, but we need to talk."

And that's when Madeline notices me hulking behind her daughter. At first, she doesn't seem to recognize me, merely tilting her head as her eyebrows draw inward with confusion. Then her memory kicks in and her mouth forms into a small "o" before she breathes out, "Kynan."

"Madeline," I return politely with a nod of my head.

I wait to see how she lets this play out. She has no clue what we know, and it's a good opportunity to just take full responsibility before things get ugly.

I'm totally disappointed when she tries to play dumb for a bit, though. "Well... this is certainly a pleasant surprise. Why don't you both come in, and we can do some catching up?"

Madeline moves back to let us in, bending over to put the small dog on the ground. It immediately runs up to me, sniffing at my leg. Ignoring it, I follow Joslyn and Madeline into a comfortable living room filled with masculine leather furniture and game trophies on the wood-paneled walls.

"Would either of you like a drink?" Madeline graciously offers, but I can hear the worry in her voice. She's banking on the one-in-a-million chance Joslyn and I have reconciled without finding out about her perfidy.

Joslyn doesn't want to draw this out. She merely states, "We know, Mom. That you gave me fake information about Kynan to make us breakup."

I brace, expecting Madeline to start trying to lie her way out of this, but to my surprise, her face crumbles.

She walks to Joslyn, grabs her hands, and squeezes them hard. "I am so sorry, honey. I knew this might come to haunt me one day, and I prayed it never would. I have no excuse other than I thought I was doing what was best for your career."

Frankly, it's the best thing Madeline could have said, and I know it's the truth. Hell, Joslyn does, too. We know she had tunnel vision when it came to her daughter's path to show business, and there's probably nothing she wouldn't have done for her.

Doesn't make it right, though.

Joslyn pulls her hands away from her mother before laying into her. "What was best for my career? Did you ever even think about what was best for me as a person? Did you ever even once consider Kynan may have been what was best for me?"

Madeline's eyes fill with tears, and she gives a slow shake of her head. "I didn't. Not once. I thought because I was older and I was your mom, I knew best. I realize that's not the case now. You see... I've learned some things these last few years since I quit managing you. I've found happiness again with Darren. I know my priorities were skewed."

"Ugh," Joslyn blurts with frustration, turning away from her mom. "Why do you have to be so insightful now? And so damn accepting of responsibility?"

I get where she's coming from. Joslyn wanted this to be a little harder on her mom. She wanted to have the right to get rid of the rest of her anger, much of it I bet still directed squarely at me for last night. Instead, her mom is rolling over and baring her throat for Joslyn to move in for the kill.

"I am so sorry, Jos," her mother says as she clasps her hands tightly in front of her chest. "I'm so sorry I hurt you. And Kynan."

I blink in surprise as Madeline turns my way. "I'm sorry, Kynan. I can't imagine how hard that was for you... to have Joslyn cut you off without any real explanation. And then to find out years later, she thought the worst about you for something you didn't do."

"I accept your apology, Madeline," I say without reservation or further judgment. Frankly, I didn't need her bloody apology. Doesn't make me feel any different about things, but I want the attention off me. I want her to resolve these things with her daughter so we can move past this.

"What's going on in here?" I hear a man's voice coming from a doorway that leads into what looks like a large dining room.

I turn to see Darren Dawes. He's a large, beefy man with snowy-white hair and a wind-weathered face. This is a guy who still clearly rides the range as he's got on jeans, chaps, and a lamb's wool jacket of a dark brown suede.

Madeline has tears slipping silently down her face, and Joslyn appears unsure of herself with Darren entering the conversation. I decide to do something rash and totally out of character for myself.

I step up to Madeline, then put my hand on her shoulder. "You and Joslyn need to talk. With your permission, I'd like to take Darren out for a beer. I'll fill him in on what's happened, and you and Joslyn can clear the air."

Several different emotions flit through Madeline's eyes as she stares back, but the most identifiable is gratitude. She gives me a nod with a watery smile before turning to her husband to introduce us. I'm able to get a brief glance at Joslyn.

She regards me with a gratefulness I hope signifies she might be willing to forgive me for last night.

"How about we just go into my study and have some bourbon?" Darren suggests.

"Works for me, mate," I reply.

He moves to his wife to kiss her on the cheek, then whispers something in her ear. She puts her hand on his and pats it before turning to Joslyn with resolve on her face. I have a feeling that things are going to get aired out nicely between the women. If Madeline is smart, she'll just let Joslyn rail a bit and get it out of her system.

CHAPTER 14

Joslyn

DARREN GIVES ME a long look of curiosity before he turns for his study. I attempt a smile, but it's weak. I know he wants me to reassure him with one look that everything is okay, but he's clearly walked into a situation that's not. His loyalty will be to my mom, as it should be, and I'm glad Kynan has urged him away from this situation. My gaze drifts over to Kynan, and I hope my eyes convey my gratitude for doing that.

It's moot, though. Kynan follows Darren out of the room without regard to me.

"I'm so very sorry, Joslyn." My mom's voice washes over me, and it's quavering with emotion.

I take in a breath and let it out slowly. Turning to face her, I lay it all out on the line, because whatever she has to say about this will determine the course of our future as a mother and daughter. "I am not going to ask 'why' because there's no mystery there. What I want to know is at what point in our relationship did I start meaning so little to you as a person and only had value to you as a means to fame and fortune?"

My mom jerks as if I'd struck her, and she shakes her head. "No, never. I never thought that. I did what I thought was best for you to push you forward to happiness. To me, the fame and fortune was your happiness. I'm not wrong about that, Joslyn. You wanted that, too, and I thought by removing the distraction I thought Kynan to be that you would appreciate it later."

She's not wrong about some of that. I did want the fame and fortune, but I wanted Kynan as well. "I could have had both with him."

"I didn't know that," she replies sadly. "In fact, I doubted it. I was nineteen once. I know how at that age, you can get consumed by another person. You hardly knew Kynan and—"

"I loved him," I interrupt her angrily. "He loved me. It was real."

"Maybe," she replies as she twists her hands. "But the chances of that being so weren't very plausible to me. I was going with the probability what you two had was too new to really matter. I had even convinced myself since Kynan didn't put up a big fight about it—that he just let you leave—that I'd done the right thing."

Damn it, I hate that her reasoning makes sense to me. Kynan just accepted it when I called it over. He obviously tried to push it when I broke it off, but he never followed up with me. Didn't keep trying. He'd given up very easily, just the way I had when I saw the photo of him hugging who I now know to be Rachel.

We both gave up, so did we even have anything real at all?

Still, it's not the point of my anger. "Mom... you didn't go about it the right way. The right way would have been to tell me your concerns. It would have been to ask for my input and make me part of the decision-making process. Instead, you lied to me. You manipulated two people. I guess what I don't understand is how you thought it was okay? Where in all of this did you actually lose your moral compass and are you still without it? Because if so, how can we ever have a real relationship?"

The expression on my mom's face morphs from one of angst and guilt to one of incredible pain. Her gaze lowers to the floor, and her voice trembles. "I'm not sure I deserve to have one with you. What I did was terrible."

She sounds broken and as if she's given up. It's then I realize while I might be terribly angry, I don't want to lose her either. I want her to fight to have something with me.

I stride across the room, then take my mom's hands in mine. Her head snaps up in surprise.

"Come here," I say as I lead her over to a burgundy overstuffed leather couch. I sit on the edge because sitting fully on the cushion would cause me to sink in, which means my legs wouldn't reach the floor. Mom follows and also mimics my pose, turning her knees into mine. I don't let go of her hands.

"I want to make this right with you, Joslyn." Her eyes are locked onto mine, her expression earnest. "Just tell me how, and I'll do it."

A sound of dismay bubbles up in my throat, and I give a mirthless laugh as I shake my head. "I have no clue what to have you do."

"Let me apologize again," she says, giving my hands a hard squeeze. "And I know I can tell you one thing… I'm not the same woman I was then. And the woman I was then—the one who set Kynan up to take a fall—wasn't the same woman you knew as your mom growing up."

"What do you mean?"

"What I mean is when your father died, you were all I had left. You weren't a child of my blood, but you were the child of my heart. There wasn't anything I wouldn't do for you, and I promised your dad on his death bed I'd always look out for you. He wanted you to be a star. I wanted that, too, for him to look down from heaven and see you get all the success you deserved."

Tears spring to my eyes, and I rub them away. "But by controlling my career, you forgot there were other things that could make me happy."

She nods, the sad frown on her face a testament she

realizes how badly she fucked up. "I didn't consider anything outside of your career. I became so focused on it, and Joslyn... I'd be lying to you if I didn't admit I liked the limelight, too. It was so easy to get swept up in it all as your manager. It gave me purpose and acknowledgment, two things I was sorely lacking after your father died. If there's one thing I'm most ashamed of, it's that some of my behavior was for my personal happiness, too. And that's why I would totally understand if you didn't forgive me. It's really inexcusable what I did."

We both stare at each other through watery eyes. I can't detect a single note of duplicity in her voice. She didn't try to excuse her actions but owned up to full responsibility. Sure... I doubt if I hadn't shown up on her doorstep, she would have brought this up herself, but really... who would? It's so easy to just steep in guilt and let it lie under the blanket of denial than to own up to your mistakes. It's human nature.

Leaning in, I move my hands to her shoulders and give her the truest words I ever said. "I forgive you."

"Really?" she asks on a half-sob, her hands going to my wrists. "Because I'd understand it if you didn't, but it would mean the world if you did."

"Really," I answer. "I understand why you did it, and you've accepted responsibility. I really believe you're remorseful. How could I ever disrespect such genuineness?"

"I love you, Joslyn," she practically moans, then falls into me where we hug long and hard.

"I love you, too."

We stay that way for a moment, but then she gives a little jolt. Pulling back, she regards me with her head tilted to the side. "But what brought you and Kynan back together?"

She puts enough emphasis on the word "together," I can see she's totally misread the nature of our current relationship.

I also know, as my mother, she's not going to like the reason why we reconnected.

"I needed some protection services," I begin, but she knows too much about my career. She managed it for many years.

"Plenty of good companies are in Los Angeles for you to hire," she says. "Why Kynan?"

"I needed the best," I reply softly. "And I needed someone I could trust."

"How could you trust him when you thought he'd cheated on you?"

It's a fair question, and one I actually asked myself when I made the decision to reach out to him. It was part gut instinct but also part of it was our history. We'd spent a lot of time talking about his career in the Royal Marines and why he came to work for Jerico Jameson. It was his passion to protect others, and I knew how much it meant to him.

"My life was—is—in serious danger," I start, ignoring her gasp of shock and the way her hand covers her mouth. "I knew Kynan very well, Mom. I know you think our connection was tenuous, but you forget how much time we spent together while he was assigned to be my guard. More time than most people spend together. We talked a lot. I knew he was the man for the job."

"What is going on, Jos?" she whispers fearfully.

"I've got a stalker, and he managed to break into my house earlier this week. He attacked me—"

"Darren," my mom yells as she bolts up from the couch. And then she yells louder, almost to the point of a screech. "Darren... get in here."

I hear the study door open so hard it slams against the doorstop, and Darren comes stampeding into the living room with fear and fury on his face. It's totally fueled by the panic in my mom's cries, but I still jump up from the couch, wanting to put myself on equal footing.

Kynan is right behind Darren. Without having the benefit of knowing my mom and I worked out our issues regarding her deceit, he stands poised to take Darren down if need be until he can figure out what's going on.

My mom points a shaky finger. "She's in danger. Someone attacked her."

Shoulders sagging in relief that something isn't physically wrong with my mom, Darren nods. "Kynan was just starting to fill me in. But are you and your girl good?"

Mom nods and steps into me, an arm going around my waist. I thought it might be a little too much given how fresh off the anger I've just come, but I guess talking about my stalker has made me feel vulnerable, so it actually feels good.

"I think we're good," my mom says hesitantly.

I confirm it, so we can move on. "Yeah… we're good."

Not great, but I think we're in a better place than we were before I showed up on her doorstep. We had never gotten back quite right after I released her as my manager. There was a void there, but I feel like that's all been bridged now with our very painful but honest talk.

"I'd like to know what the hell is going on with my daughter, though," my mom says with her eyes lasered onto Kynan.

"Here's the deal," Kynan says calmly, and we all swivel his way.

He then proceeds to tell my mom and stepfather all about my stalker and what he's done so far, which causes my mom to cry. Darren moves to her, then pulls her down onto the couch where she can sink into his embrace. I move over to one of the overstuffed chairs, also in burgundy leather, as Kynan proceeds to tell them about our game plan to draw this man out.

"I don't like this," my mom proclaims. "You can't use Joslyn as bait."

"I won't let anything happen to her," Kynan replies. The deep rumble of commitment in his voice is reassuring to me. I can tell by the look on my mom's face that it does nothing to ease her.

"Mom," I say, and her gaze drifts to me. "If we don't do this, then it's just a wait-and-see game to him. It could be weeks. Months. I can't go on that long looking around every corner waiting for him to spring out at me."

My mom seems to consider this, and she gives her attention to Darren. He nods back as if this makes good sense.

"I need this done now," I tell my mom, glancing over at Kynan who is leaning up against one of the walls. "I want this done so I can get my life back. Besides, I can't keep Kynan around forever."

Kynan flinches slightly, but I pay it no mind. I'm sure he'd rather get back to his life as well.

"Well, we can talk about this some more over dinner—"

I cut my mom off by standing up. "We really can't stay, Mom. We didn't even pack an overnight bag and we took a private jet, which is on standby for us to return tonight. On top of that, we're scheduled to do our relationship 'reveal' on the Cara Peterson show the day after tomorrow. We really have a lot to do to get ready for that."

"Joslyn, please," my mom pleads. She's fearful for me, and she's trying to hold tight now to alleviate those worries.

"We really can't," I state sorrowfully, really wishing I could stay for one of her home-cooked meals. Like the kind she used to make when I was younger—before she started worrying about whether it all went to my hips.

My mom sighs long and heavy. It hits the mark, and I feel guilty.

That interaction is what makes me think we'll be okay.

CHAPTER 15

Kynan

"**Y**OU'RE UP EARLY," I comment to Rachel as I walk into Joslyn's kitchen. She's sitting at the center island, cup of coffee in front of her. Bebe is to her left, tapping away on her computer as they both study the screen.

"Went for a run," Rachel replies. "But come over here and take a look… Bebe's just uploaded the video I got from that flower shop yesterday."

While Joslyn and I had flown to Cunningham Falls so she could hash it out with her mom, Rachel had gone to the shop where we believe the stalker purchased the sunflowers. They indeed had security video, but the owner wasn't in and was the only one who could authorize the information to be released to Rachel. She had to wait around until late afternoon, and then the owner proved to be quite the bugger. He couldn't be convinced to turn the footage over out of the goodness of his heart to help catch a sick fuck who tried to murder someone. He did, however, respond to the color green.

Eventually, Rachel negotiated a payment of two thousand dollars in return for a flash drive with the security footage.

I grab a cup, pour some coffee, and walk around the island to come up behind Bebe and Rachel.

"Here we go," Bebe says, then the footage of the inside of the flower shop starts to roll. The camera is set up in a corner, behind the register and facing outward to the interior of the shop through to the glass entrance door. The imagery is grayscale, and the quality just a tad better than overly grainy.

"Go to 11:47 on the video," Rachel tells Bebe, who then uses the scroll bar to advance the footage forward.

"There," Rachel exclaims, and Bebe slows the footage to regular speed.

At first, all I see is a female customer perusing a shelf of knickknacks. The flower shop is what I'd expect. A big cooler of premade arrangements on one wall. Shelves with overpriced trinkets.

"There he is," Rachel murmurs as the glass door opens. A blond man of medium height and build walks in. Everything about him is nondescript except for the fact he's wearing his sunglasses inside. He doesn't bother to remove them or push them onto his head. He's wearing jeans and a long-sleeved shirt despite the warmth of the day, and that tells me he might have an identifying mark he's trying to conceal. Maybe a birth mark or tattoo.

He strides up to the counter to talk to the shop employee there. They have an incredibly brief conversation before she steps out of camera range, presumably to a back room. We watch in silence as the time stamp ticks away. About fifteen minutes later, the woman comes back with the exact style of flower arrangement—sunflowers—that was found at the edge of Joslyn's property.

"That's him for sure," Rachel says.

"Indeed," I mutter, then nod to the screen. "Play it again."

Bebe rewinds it, and the three of us watch again. I notice a few things. The man is smart enough to keep his face angled away from the camera. The oversized aviators he's wearing hide a nice chunk of his face, but his refusal to face the camera head-on tells me he's aware of the camera's position and knows the power of the more advanced facial recognition software out there. What he doesn't know is I don't have the exact product yet, but I'm getting an advanced version that's being created right now by the Defense Intelligence Agency. Until then, I'll have to send this video off for scanning, but I doubt we'd get anything useful because the guy is being overly cautious.

While he waits for the arrangement to be made, he pulls out a phone and surfs on it, turning fully away from the camera. He pays for the arrangement in cash and then leaves.

"Once again," I tell Bebe, but in truth, I'll probably watch this video a good dozen times before I'm satisfied I've gleaned all the necessary information from it.

It starts once more, and Rachel moves from her stool to the coffee pot for a refill. I lean inward to get a better look.

"Is that him?" Joslyn's voice hits me from behind, and it sounds a little gruff as if she'd just woken up. Sure enough, when I twist, she's there in a silk robe that hits just above her knees with her hair a wild mess. She looks utterly fuckable.

Stepping back slightly, I motion her forward to have a closer look. She does, wrapping her arms protectively around her stomach as she watches the video. When it gets to the part where the employee leaves to make the arrangement and he turns away from the camera even more to surf on his phone, I ask Joslyn, "Do you recognize him?"

Her eyes don't leave the screen, but she gives a slight shake of her head. Her voice is soft and tentative. "He was wearing a ski mask."

I already knew that. Besides, it wasn't really what I was seeking. I was wondering if there an overall recognition she felt upon seeing him, especially if she'd seen him somewhere else and hadn't known who it was.

But I don't push her on it.

"I never understood that," she murmurs, her eyes still riveted on Bebe's computer screen.

"What's that?" Bebe asks.

"Why he'd wear a mask to kill me." My skin turns cold from her words. "I mean... not like I could identify him, right?"

"He was worried about you having security cameras in your house," I answer, resisting the urge to put a protective arm around her. I want to pull her into my side so she knows I will handle every single vulnerability she's feeling right now and make it all go away.

She nods, a slight acknowledgment she hears me as she continues watching the video. We're all silent, Rachel staying on the other side of the counter as she sips her coffee. The video ends, and I don't ask Bebe to replay it as I don't want Joslyn to look at him anymore.

"Onions," she says as her eyes stay glued to the laptop.

"Onions?" I ask.

She turns to me, her nose wrinkling in distaste. "His breath smelled like onions. And burnt coffee. And I think in ordinary circumstances, it would have made me sick, but I was so scared I didn't even have time to be sick."

Bloody hell, but that slays me. Knowing she thought her life was going to end. I'd been in that scenario before, and it's a fear that's almost indescribable.

"I was raped," Bebe says quietly, and my lungs practically deflate at the sudden proclamation. I don't recall anything in her file about that, so I have to assume it went unreported.

All heads turn to her way, except Joslyn steps in closer and puts a light hand on Bebe's shoulder in sympathy. Jos's face is pained, but Bebe's eyes are clear and her voice is strong as she gives a reassuring smile. "My attacker's eyes were bloodshot. I don't know if maybe he was lacking in sleep or maybe he was on drugs, but for the longest time, I would have nightmares about those bloodshot eyes. Except in my dreams, they weren't naturally red. More like supernaturally red. My point in telling you that is I can promise—over a period of time—those memories will lessen significantly as you process and deal. I can't say you'll ever let it go, but it will get easier."

Christ... now I feel the need to hug Bebe, but I restrain myself. Besides, Joslyn beats me to the punch and leans over to wrap the woman in her arms. "I'm sorry that happened to you. Thank you for sharing that."

Bebe gives a slight shrug as Joslyn pulls back. "It's nothing. I put it behind me long ago."

While her words are strong and her tone staunch, there's something dark in her eyes that makes me doubt it. Bebe's been through a lot in the last several years.

Blackmailed, arrested, and sent to prison, raped at some point in that time frame.

Torn from her son.

I make a mental note to talk to Dr. Ellery about Bebe. I don't have any doubts about my hiring of her, but the rape is an added element I need to keep at the forefront of my mind. I don't want to put her in any scenario that could be harmful to her psyche.

Smiling, Joslyn looks around the kitchen at us. "How about I make breakfast for everyone? French toast?"

"Sounds delicious," Rachel agrees lightheartedly. "Then Bebe and I have to get packed."

"Packed?" Joslyn asks as she moves around the island to where Rachel is standing. She brushes by her to reach into the cup cabinet so she can fix her coffee. "Where are you two going?"

"Back to Vegas," I answer on their behalf. "Rachel has to get back to running the office there, and I'm going to have Bebe go there until we get the Pittsburgh office up and running."

What I don't say out loud is I've arranged for Bebe's mother and son to meet her in Vegas for a reunion next week. I know she's been in phone contact with them, but since she's jumped right into this case with Joslyn, it's sort of put her family on the back burner. I want her to get reintegrated into society and family life as quickly as possible. That's going to go a long way toward her healing.

"Well, I'll send you off with your bellies full at least," Joslyn quips as she turns for the refrigerator. "It's the least I can do for everything you've done for me."

Both Rachel and Bebe smile at Joslyn with a natural fondness that's developed quite quickly between the women. I wonder when this is all over and done, will Joslyn remain friends with them?

With me?

I mean, surely there's at least that when we eliminate the threat.

Right?

I don't know the answer to that. Even if the answer were yes—that we could still be friends—it bothers me more than I care to admit I'm wholly unsatisfied with that.

CHAPTER 16

Joslyn

HARRY WALKS INTO my bedroom with Lynn following along behind him. He's got three large wardrobe boxes in his arms, which he gently sits on the end of my bed. "There... all three of these outfits are stunning, but my recommendation is to go with the Alexis Mabille. The blue will make your eyes pop on camera."

Harry and Lynn have come over today to do preparation for my appearance on Cara Peterson tomorrow. I've been a little out of sorts since Bebe and Rachel left about an hour ago, and I've been hiding in my bedroom ever since. Kynan set up a temporary office in my kitchen. I feel like I'm intruding if I go in there, or even the great room into which the kitchen naturally bleeds. I didn't realize how much of a buffer Bebe and Rachel were between Kynan and me until they were gone. But the minute we watched their Uber pull away to take them to LAX and Kynan reset the alarm to lock us securely inside, I felt completely vulnerable without them.

Not that I'm in danger with Kynan or he would hurt me, but that we might have to actually talk about the issues between us. After we left my mom's last night and flew back from Cunningham Falls, Kynan has admittedly been a lot easier to get along with. He's tried to make small talk with me, and he hasn't even glared once. He seems to be over his anger about me not trusting him more twelve years ago, and I also feel the slap I gave him was really all the retaliation I needed.

Still... it makes things confusing now, especially because if I've learned one thing since Kynan has come back into my life it's that I remember just how easy it is to love a man like that. I simply can't afford to let my heart get broken again, ergo... I'm hiding in my room.

"You try those on," Harry instructs me. "I'm going to go make some calls from your office and work on the finishing touches of the press release that's going out after Cara's show goes live."

Cara tapes in front of a national audience, and our interview won't go live until tomorrow morning. The news outlets will pick up the story I'm now "engaged," and Harry has several more interviews for me throughout the week—both on camera and via phone. There's a large part of me that hates this ruse I'm perpetrating on my fans, and I can only hope they will forgive me once we catch this stalker and they know the reasons why I'm doing what I'm doing.

"I'd have rather gone out shopping," I mutter as I put my phone down on the nightstand and pull my legs up. Wrapping my arms around my shins, I tell Harry pointedly, "Thank you for doing this for me."

"It was no big deal," he says airily, and then breezes out of my room.

Normally, I would relish the chance to go shopping with Harry and Lynn. We'd hit a few boutique stores on Melrose before going out for lunch. It's one of the best things about living in this area and I actually don't do it often, so it's a great treat.

But Kynan nixed the idea of us going out shopping. He said it wasn't safe. I told him it was if he was with me, to which he replied, "I've got other things I need to do that take priority. You'll just have to stay here."

I wasn't happy about that. I'm a prisoner in my own home, and I've never had my freedom curtailed this way. At least, not since before I met Kynan and my mom was "managing" me.

I'm not sure what expression my face held when Kynan told me I couldn't go, but before I could even take a breath, he'd drawn me into his arms for a protective, sympathetic embrace. I was stiff and held my arms to my side at first, not understanding a damn thing about what was happening. But Kynan just wrapped his arms around me, squeezed gently, and kissed the top of my head ever so gently. He then murmured, "I know this is hard on you, Jos. It will be over soon, though. I promise."

I succumbed. My arms went around his waist, and I let him hug me. I let him envelop me in his strength, and I relished in the comfort and security.

"What if this drags on?" I asked while pressing my cheek into his chest and trying not to notice how great he smelled. "What if he doesn't come after me right away? You have a new business you're trying to get up and running. I know you can't stay here forever."

Kynan's chest rumbled with an easygoing laugh. "Then I'll have to cart you off to Pittsburgh with me, I guess."

I didn't tell him that was a ludicrous notion, even though it absolutely is. I didn't press him for a better answer. Instead, I let my mind wander for just a moment about what it would be like to leave this life and start over again somewhere else.

With Kynan.

My musings were cut short, though, when Kynan released me. I coughed to clear my throat, turning away so he couldn't see my red face. I muttered something like, "I'm sure it will all work out for the best."

I then retreated to my room, called Lynn, who called Harry, who then went shopping for me.

And here they are.

Lynn steps further into my room, then plops down

on my bed. "Save yourself the time and just go with Harry's suggestion."

I chuckle, crawling onto my bed to sit opposite of Lynn. Eyeballing the boxes, I decide to take her advice. Harry's got better taste than I do.

"Saw Kynan working in the kitchen," Lynn remarks as she pulls her legs up and crosses them Indian-style. "He said Bebe and Rachel left to go back to Vegas."

With a nod, I mimic her movement. I pick at a piece of nonexistent lint on my yoga pants. "Feels weird with them gone, even though they were only here for a few days."

"And now you're forced to deal with Kynan," Lynn quips, and my head snaps up in astonishment.

"What do you mean?" I ask, trying to sound nonchalant, but there's a level of hysteria in my voice.

Lynn rolls her eyes. Such kind eyes most of the time. Lynn has become a second mother figure to me after I let my own mother go as my manager. She shakes her head, which is covered with a short cap of the most luxurious premature silver hair I'd ever seen on another human. I once tried to get her to admit to me she colored it, but she swore on her dog's life—a Yorkie named Bob—that it was her natural hair.

"Come on, Jos," she chides. "Kynan is something to you. You haven't told me what, and I've tried to mind my own business, but since we're sitting here talking and all… why don't you just go ahead and spill it?"

"I don't know what you mean," I reply lamely, dropping my gaze so I'm not looking directly at her as I lie.

"Joslyn." Her tone is low and warning in nature. "Don't even think to bullshit me. I see the way that man looks at you. You have your head stuck in the sand most of the time when it comes to men. Half the time, he looks at you like he's seen a ghost come back to life. The other half, it's with a hunger that actually makes me fear for you. In a good kind of way, you know?"

Her words send a tremble up my spine. "Really?"

"Really," she replies with a firm nod. "So what's the deal with you two?"

I stare a moment, wondering if I should tell her about the real story between us. Because if I do, I'm going to have to tell her about my jumbled-up feelings. Once I do that, it becomes real.

Ultimately, I open my mouth and the story just comes pouring out. I told her about how my mom insisted on hiring his company to protect me even though I thought it was stupid, but that once he'd been assigned to me, I quickly changed my mind. How we spent so much time alone together, hours just talking about everything under the sun. I told her with no shame about the attraction, but we didn't act upon it because he was a professional and I was too inexperienced to know how to make a move. But once we did come together, the fireworks we produced were shattering to me. No one since has come close to replicating those feelings.

I also told her how we ended, and how, just recently, we realized my mother's role in deceiving us both.

"Oh wow," Lynn murmurs. "That's why you went to Cunningham Falls yesterday?"

I nod.

"This is wonderful, though." She sighs dreamily. I even get a sappy smile from her. "It's your second chance at love."

"No, it's not," I snap so fast she jerks her chin inward as her eyes widen. Calming my tone, I shake my head. "It's just... there's too much anger there, and we're totally different people now. I mean... he's a one-night stand kind of guy and I'm all about commitment."

"Bullshit," Lynn replies.

"Excuse me? What's bullshit?"

"That you're a commitment type of person," she says blandly. "You've not had a relationship last longer than six months. You always break it off when things get too serious."

I open my mouth immediately to argue with her, but it snaps shut just as quickly as I realize she's right. I shy away from the type of feelings that could lead to heartbreak. Still, I won't outright admit that. I merely say, "I just haven't found the right person yet. If I did, then I'm all for commitment."

"Or maybe you have found the right one." The expression on her face is sly and mischievous.

"No way," I deny. "Too much hurt. No way we could work it out."

"Or you could say it's water under the bridge and take a shot."

"No," I reply with an adamant shake of my head. "Besides... Kynan hasn't been so quick to forgive me. Even though my mom orchestrated the false investigative report, he's got some hard feelings for the fact I didn't trust him enough."

"How do you know?" she asks lightly. "Have you talked?"

Something like that, I think. I'm not about to tell her about our sexcapades and the way he left me so abruptly.

True, Kynan's playing nice and professional now, and we've seemingly put that behind us, but I know what I did is probably unforgivable in the long run.

CHAPTER 17

Kynan

I HAVE THE freedom to watch Joslyn, and she has no clue. She's stuck in a chair at a dressing table, her makeup and hair being done by two separate people. I'm off to the side where she can't see me in the mirror's reflection, and I'm enjoying the view.

It brings me back twelve years ago when she was in Vegas. I'd sat in her dressing room on many occasions while she was being made up to surpass the perfection she already was. Her bubbly personality always shined bright as she horsed around before she was set to go on stage. She and her stylist always cracked jokes, mostly too stupid to even remember, but I loved how purely effervescent she was to be around.

My memory hitches a bit and then falters as I recollect those days.

"Hey," I say, interrupting the chatter of the makeup and hair stylists working on her. "What happened to your stylist in Vegas? I can't remember his name."

Joslyn's hair is currently held hostage in an iron, so

she can't turn around, but I can see the side of her jaw. Her dimple pops, which means she's smiling. "Michel."

"That's right, Michel," I reminisce. "He was a bloody hoot."

"He's still back in Vegas," she replies with a laugh. "Married and has two kids."

"No kidding," I say, fondly remembering the overly exuberant, extremely dramatic, but anti-relationship gay man.

"Yup. Married a really nice guy," Joslyn says. "A tow-truck driver, believe it or not."

Chuckling, I shake my head over the fact it actually doesn't surprise me at all. "Vegas has everything."

It's the first time in a long time I've been able to think back on my time with Joslyn and not be offended by it. Hell, the memories are actually producing warm and fuzzy feelings for the first time in forever.

And maybe it's because the stroll down memory lane has me feeling slightly nostalgic, and I don't want to have to think about Joslyn going on national TV soon to tell the world we're a couple. It's not that I mind the attention. Never been a shy bloke.

But after this show is done taping, then it's game on. Her stalker—if the plan works right—is going to make a showing. I hope it's sooner rather than later. The longer this goes on, the more stressed Jos is going to become. Besides that, I have a life I need to get back to and I'd be lying if I didn't say being around her is difficult.

I have to admit I'm not angry at her anymore. I've reminded myself she was nineteen and under her mother's control for a long time. While I am solid with the fact I loved her and she loved me, I also know a young girl confronted with seemingly legit evidence of my betrayal would be affected differently than she would today at age thirty-two with some experience behind her. I have to forgive Joslyn for not knowing any better.

And the minute I did that, I sure as fuck started itching to have her again. Just hugging her yesterday in her kitchen felt so goddamn great I could've just been happy standing there for hours. Bloody hell, but feelings have resurfaced for me and it's a mind fuck for sure. I'm getting ready to let her perpetuate a lie to the world that we're in love, except it doesn't feel like a complete and utter lie to me.

More importantly, we have got to sell this if her stalker is going to believe it. I need him to believe so he gets pissed—hopefully sloppy—and decides to come after her so I can end the bloody ponce.

This job has become way too personal now. What I really want is for Joslyn to have peace and be happy again.

The makeup artist finishes and leaves the room. After a few more fluffs of Joslyn's hair, the hair stylist leaves and it's time for Joslyn to get dressed. She brought a light blue dress the same color as her eyes and a pair of high-heeled booties in a camel color to wear with it. It's hanging on a hook beside the mirror. Joslyn pushes out of her chair, nabbing the outfit. She raises a brow pointedly. "Want to step out while I get dressed?"

I smile slowly, a silent admission I've seen everything she has to show me. She glares and I merely turn, giving her my back. "We need to talk so go ahead and get dressed. I promise not to peek."

She makes a delicate snort that has me grinning bigger, but then I hear the unmistakable sound of her removing her jeans. The distinct sound of the zipper coming down makes my blood turn hot.

Shaking my head, I put that aside. "Look… you have got to sell this out there. To the audience."

"I know," she says with a resigned sigh. "They need to believe we're in love."

"No," I say sharply, then turn my head just enough I can see her in my peripheral vision. She freezes in her panties and bra, eyes wide. "*He* has to believe it. He has to watch this interview, and he has to become enraged. So you have to do more than sell it, Joslyn. It's going to be the biggest acting role of your career."

"I've got this," she snaps, and it's enough to prompt me to face her.

"Do you?" I taunt, trying my damned best not to ogle her. A quick glimpse of her body in that sexy-as-fuck white lace lingerie is seared onto my brain. "Because things are kind of strained between us."

"Well, yeah," she snarls in outrage, completely glorious in her near nudity as she stares daggers. "I'm a little ragey still that you fucked me and then treated me like garbage after."

"Joslyn—"

"I let you into my body, Kynan," she seethes, and I realize she's had some buried fury she's been keeping deep under wraps with me. I don't interrupt her—just let her get it out. "That wasn't a whim for me, and I wasn't acting on just pure sexual attraction. I fell right back into it with you the minute I realized you hadn't betrayed me, and all you wanted to do was bust a nut. So I'm sorry if I'm having a tough time coping, but please rest assured… I'll sell our fake little love story. I'm actually quite good at what I do."

Joslyn stands there, chest heaving with indignation, but I can also see relief she managed to get that out. She clearly needed to.

"You're wrong about one thing." My voice is soft, noncombative. I need to ease her off the ledge. We have less than ten minutes before she has to go on national TV.

"What's that?" she asks, her head tilted curiously.

"It wasn't just about busting a nut with you. I left you because I was angry and in emotional overload over just how fucking amazing it felt to be with you again. Give me a little credit why don't you? Maybe I was just as overwhelmed as you by everything I'd learned, and I just didn't handle it very well."

"Oh," Joslyn breathes, as if she just had an epiphany. Then it dawns on her what I said, and she lets out an even longer, "O-h-h-h."

I take two steps, come right before her, and put my hands on her shoulders. Bending slightly, I look right into her eyes. "I think you and I have things to talk about. But the one thing I need you to know is I'm not angry with you anymore over what happened. It's in the past and I'm letting it go, okay?"

She nods, worrying her lower lip with her teeth. There are all kinds of things I'd like to do with her lip. Instead, I ask, "Let's both put that bad stuff behind us. Okay, Jos?"

"Okay," she murmurs in agreement.

It's nothing for me to lean into her and press my lips to her forehead briefly. I only pull away because there's a short knock on the door.

Turning from Joslyn, I head to the door and open it. A young woman holding an iPad with a headset on says, "Miss Meyers goes on in ten. Anything else I can get for her?"

I shake my head. "We're good."

The woman beams and leaves.

When I turn, Joslyn has the blue dress on and is sitting in the vanity chair, putting on her high-heeled booties. While I liked her better in her lingerie, there's no denying she is the most exquisite creature I've ever known in my life. Her pale blond hair is in multi-layered waves down her back, and her eyes are dark and smoky. The dress is sleeveless, low cut, and fits her like a glove. She is sex personified. Yet, she also looks like an angel at the same time.

She zips the last boot and stands, smoothing her dress. "Do I look okay?"

"You're more beautiful than any woman I've ever known," I respond.

Joslyn blushes, her cheeks and chest turning a rosy red. Her eyes sparkle, and she looks nineteen again.

♦

STANDING IN THE wings of the studio stage for *The Cara Peterson Show*, I watch Joslyn as she talks about her album that's in production now. Sitting on a couch angled to an overstuffed chair where the host is settled, Joslyn is the epitome of style, beauty, and grace.

Can't say as I've ever watched *The Cara Peterson Show*, but her name is recognizable even to me, so she's clearly got the reach we need. The audience went crazy when Joslyn was introduced a few minutes ago. I sweep my eyes over the people staring up with smiles on their faces, and it's apparent just how much she's loved.

I don't have to worry about her stalker being in the audience. These tickets were pre-sold weeks ago. Harry managed to pull a miracle and get her slipped into the guest lineup. I assume that means someone got bumped, but it's not my problem.

"So what do you love more, Joslyn?" Cara asks. She's an attractive woman in her late forties who transitioned from national network news to her own talk show about a decade ago. "Creating films or music?"

"Without a doubt... music," Joslyn replies instantly with a slight chuckle. It's obvious she gets this question a lot. "While acting is challenging and rewarding, my music comes from my soul. And to share it with others is something indescribable. Writing and performing songs will be my first love. Always."

"Speaking of love," Cara says mysteriously, casting a sly look out at the audience before turning back to Joslyn. My body tenses because here it comes. Cara was filled in on the issue of Joslyn's stalker, and she was prepared to set up the reveal about me. "I've heard a rumor you've got a new beau in your life."

For a brief, stunning moment, I want that statement to be true more than I want anything else. I shake it off, focusing in on the conversation.

When the audience starts cheering, Joslyn gives them a shy smile before being coy with Cara. "You might say that."

"You've notoriously shied away from relationships," Cara says, and that's news to me. While I've loosely followed Joslyn's career, I've never watched entertainment shows or read tabloids… those news sources where I'd find out about those sorts of things. I didn't want to know about any of that.

"I've always put my career first," Joslyn replies with a laugh. "Not necessarily shied away."

Cara inclines her head graciously, although it's clear she doesn't believe that. From her demeanor, I realize the Hollywood gossip mill must take Joslyn Meyers being in a relationship as a big deal.

"Rumor is…" Cara presses on. "That you're in a relationship and it's the real deal."

The audience goes nuts, screaming and cheering. People start calling out, "Who is it?"

Whether it's an act or not, Joslyn comes off embarrassed. She waves playfully at the audience, and Cara pushes once again. "Well… tell us. Clearly, this is huge news."

Joslyn tilts her head back and laughs. Her eyes are sparkling with amusement, and it's a mighty fine acting job. "Okay, okay… I'll tell you."

Cara motions for the audience to quiet down. Once they do, Joslyn leans toward Cara. "Okay… so I reconnected recently with my first love. My only love, actually. And well… let's just say the sparks flew again."

"And are you going to tell us who the lucky man is? A Hollywood heartthrob? A rock star?"

Laughing, Joslyn shakes her head. "Actually… he owns a security company. I've recently been in need of his services. It's been years, but I reached out to him and he agreed to take my case. From there…well, nature just happened."

That's good.

Really good.

Once her stalker sees this, it's going to piss him off to know his own actions caused our reconnection. But will it be enough to provoke him?

"Why do you need security?" Cara asks.

Joslyn tries for a game smile, but it falters. Her voice rasps a bit when she explains, "I have a stalker. Things have gotten pretty bad. Well… I just feel safer with protection."

"That's awful," Cara croons, and the audience murmurs their assent.

Joslyn manages a bit of a brighter smile.

"What's your new fella's name?" Cara—going back to her reporter instincts—prods with a gleam to her eye.

"Would you like to meet him?" Joslyn asks, and my body locks tight. This was most definitely not in the plan, but as Joslyn grins at me where I'm standing in the wings, I can see a devilish quirk to her lips.

Cara turns to ask the audience. "Would we?"

A deafening cheer rises, and Joslyn stands from the couch. She smiles across the way, motioning with her hand for me to come join her.

I vow to myself if I get her back in bed, I'm going to spank her ass until it's red as a fire engine. But for now, I decide to go with the flow. I'd dressed casually in a pair of jeans, a t-shirt, and a blazer, so it's with confidence I step out into the spotlight. A stagehand quickly mics me up.

I grin at the audience as I throw them a wave. Turning to Joslyn, I lock my eyes on her as I head her way. Moving past Cara I give a small nod of my head, but then my attention returns to Joslyn.

My pace doesn't slow. I walk right into her, a hand going behind her head and another to her waist. My mouth crashes down on hers, a bit more punishing than necessary, but that's payback for calling me out here like that. Still, the reward of her tongue slashing against mine as I bend her backward with the force of my kiss is everything.

When I let her up, I vaguely hear Cara say, "Oh wow… now that's a kiss."

Joslyn stares with eyes wide with astonishment, but also sizzling with heat. She felt that kiss between her legs if I was a betting man.

As the crowd's applause starts to die, Joslyn does a

quick introduction to Cara and then I'm sitting on the couch next to Joslyn. I toss my arm over the back of the couch and let my fingers graze softly over the bare skin on her upper arm, hiding my satisfied grin when Joslyn shivers in response.

To my surprise—and oddly, my delight because this is just a ruse after all—she shimmies in closer to my body until her side is plastered to me.

"So, Kynan," Cara drawls from her chair, boldly eyeballing me. "You're a security professional?"

I give her an incline of my head in acknowledgment. "I own a company called Jameson Force Security and—"

I'm interrupted by Cara audibly swooning and the audience gasping. Confused, I watch Cara, who is fanning herself and staring at Joslyn. "You didn't tell us he's British. Oh my God… that accent."

I don't even know what to say, but Cara winks at the audience. "Am I right, ladies? Like who wouldn't fall in love with that voice?"

I'm actually disappointed in myself when a warm flush creeps up my neck. I mean… I'm all for the ladies ogling me or whatever the fuck it is they do, but it's Joslyn's tiny giggle from beside me that has me staring down at her. She peeks up through long lashes and just shrugs, her amusement evident.

But I don't want to waste time or opportunity, since the message we came to convey needs to be said. I smile rakishly at Cara, but my eyes are hard with determination. "Don't go swooning over me. I'm totally taken by this woman here. Like she said... she hired me to protect her from a particularly cowardly ponce who thinks he can terrorize her."

It's here I glare directly into the camera, laying down my challenge. "And if he's watching, I have a message. If he comes near my fiancée again, he'll regret it."

This is so far off script from what Joslyn or Cara was anticipating, and I need to make sure this part of the interview isn't cut. If he wasn't provoked by Joslyn before, he will be now.

But that doesn't seem to be particularly important to Cara. She practically squeals, "Fiancée? You're engaged. Where's the ring? When are you going to tie the knot? You must tell us everything."

CHAPTER 18

Joslyn

"**G**O GET INTO something comfortable," Kynan says as we step inside my front door. "Do you want beer or wine?"

"Wine," I say as we move through the great room. I turn left toward my room, but Kynan goes right into the kitchen since he's carrying the pizza we'd picked up.

We had talked about going out to dinner with Lynn and Harry, both of whom were with us at *The Cara Peterson Show*, but I just didn't have it in me. Perpetrating a ruse I was engaged to my first true love was about the most mentally exhausting thing I'd done in a long time.

It wasn't so hard letting the lies come forth. The story was pretty straightforward and based so much in truth because of how we reconnected that at least it felt realistic.

The hard part was sitting there with Kynan's arm around my shoulder, his thumb tenderly rubbing against my shoulder in perhaps a show of being supportive and nurturing. He'd issued a challenge to my stalker when he'd stared right in the camera and threatened him—and Cara and the audience practically swooned.

The worst part was how genuine Kynan sounded. Cara was so taken with his British accent and his alpha-protective charm I barely was asked any other questions during the interview. It became *The Kynan McGrath Show*, and the man knows how to put on the charm. It seemed so natural and genuine when he told her how deeply he loved me all these years and how he had never been able to move on.

He was smooth when Cara asked him why we'd broken up. He waved it off to youth and stupidity and left it at that.

Kynan kissed me at the end of the segment, then he held my hand the entire way to the dressing room. I didn't even want to bother getting into my jeans, eager to put the entire thing behind me because let's face it... he sounded so convincing, my heart was starting to respond. I started wondering... could we have something?

Yeah... my head was a mess and I was tired, so I declined dinner with Lynn and Harry. Instead, I opted for my favorite pizza. Kynan was quiet as he normally tends to be, but he still held my hand the entire way out of the studio and to my car since he'd driven us to the studio in it.

He opened the passenger door for me, but before I could slide in, he put his hand around the nape of my neck and gave it a squeeze. Adding to my confusion he bent his head and murmured, "You did great, Joslyn. I think we set the trap."

His face was so close to mine. With his eyes like warm pools of concern and care, I thought he was going to kiss me for real.

But he didn't.

He merely smiled and gestured for me to get in.

Now, my current game plan is to get out of these booties because while they look killer, they are torture on my feet. After that, I'm going to remove my bra, put on a t-shirt and sweatshirt, along with my favorite pair of beat-up sweatpants, then I'm going to gorge on pizza and wine. I will hopefully drink enough I can fall into a catatonic sleep instead of playing every nuance of Kynan's words and actions over and over again.

In my bedroom, I head to my closet. It's massive and decadent, with all the clothing and shoes on the perimeter shelves. In the center, I have a free-standing square dresser with a granite top that holds my lingerie and jewelry. After plopping onto a small tufted chair inside, I take off the booties and groan as my toes sink into the plush carpeting. I sit there a moment, my mind immediately wandering to the Cara Peterson interview and the kind and loving things Kynan had said about me.

Lies, right?

With a sigh, I force myself out of the chair. I have pizza and wine waiting, so I remove my jewelry—earrings, necklace, and rings—and put them all back in their proper places.

My eye catches on a blue sapphire ring nestled in a velvet trough in one of the drawers. It's huge, emerald cut, and so big I rarely wear it. I had bought it for myself when I won my first Grammy, but that was years ago. I doubt I've worn in three times since.

I slide it onto the ring finger on my left hand. Cara Peterson had hounded Kynan once he announced we were engaged over the fact I hadn't been wearing an engagement ring. I immediately jumped to his defense, telling Cara I had chosen not to wear it until we had officially announced our engagement but since the cat was out of the bag, I'd have to put it on.

This would work.

I hold my hand out, look at the sparkling facets, and hate the deep pit of longing within the middle of my stomach. I want this for myself—not for it to be a sham.

And not necessarily with Kynan, although I suspect that might be a lie. Again, quite confused over all these feelings. It had occurred to me recently I've shied away from relationships. Lynn called me on the carpet yesterday. Truthfully, what I thought was a betrayal by the man I loved had warped the way I viewed the possibility of true love.

Or, conversely, maybe I don't believe in it and haven't since the moment I was told Kynan cheated on me.

It's been a shitty way to live, and I don't want to do it anymore.

"Pretty ring." Kynan's voice comes from my closet door. He's standing there, hands casually pushed into the front pockets of his jeans. He's removed his blazer, and the t-shirt underneath is molded superbly to his body. Both arms sport full-sleeve tattoos, and I remember being oh so turned on by them when I was younger.

That feeling hasn't changed.

Kynan's gaze moves from my face down to the ring. He nods at it, a silent prod to tell him about it.

I shrug and take it off, setting it down in the drawer. "I figure we can use it as a prop engagement ring when we're out in public."

"I'm sorry that was so hard on you today," he says, and I'm rocked to the core by the regret I can hear in his voice.

"It's okay." I shoot him a shy smile, for some reason incredibly relieved that it seems Kynan is truly done with being mad. I think part of the stress of the last few hours was knowing he was putting on such a show for the cameras but thinking under it all, he was still very much disgusted with my lack of trust in him before.

I don't hear any of that.

I hear nothing but true empathy from him, and it touches me.

"Let me get changed and we can gorge on some pizza," I say with a grin. "It cures all woes."

Kynan pulls one hand from his pocket, then makes a motion with his index finger for me to spin around. "I'll unzip your dress."

The warm rumble of words—his commanding tone—all of it hits me straight between my legs. Shaking my head to clear it, I take in a long breath. It doesn't mean a thing.

I turn away from Kynan, pulling my long hair over one shoulder to reveal the zipper. My ears strain to hear him, but he approaches me silently.

Then a large hand comes to my shoulder, warm and heavy. The other goes to the zipper, and he starts to lower it ever so slowly. He's standing close because I can feel heat coming off his body. His breath hits the nape of my neck.

Is this a seduction or is he being neighborly?

I can't help but snort at the thought, and Kynan's hand stops midway down my back. "What's so funny?"

Well, fuck… might as well be honest. I give a slight clearing of my throat. "I was just wondering if you were being neighborly by helping me with my zipper or if you were trying to seduce me?"

Kynan's voice is gentle but chiding with a hint of amusement. "If I was trying to seduce you, Jos, you'd know it. You wouldn't have to ask."

I'm immediately disappointed.

Damn it all to hell, I want him to seduce me.

"For example," he says lightly, and he touches the bare skin revealed by the opened zipper. He slowly drags a knuckle down my spine. "I would perhaps touch you like this."

My breath seems to freeze in my lungs. I hold absolutely still, even as I can feel goose bumps breaking free in the path of his grazing touch.

"Or," he continues, his tone a little lower. Rougher. "I might do this."

And then his lips are on my neck. I feel a waft of hot breath before his teeth graze over my skin, down along the slope of my shoulder. He bites me gently, then drags his tongue over the spot.

My body isn't my own. I push my hips backward into him, needing to feel his body.

And I do.

Big and hard.

Extremely hard in some places.

Kynan lifts his face, rubs his bearded cheek over mine, and whispers, "I want inside you, Joslyn."

Part of me is relieved by his words, because they're carnal and rooted in the need for release. There's nothing wrong with that. I want it, too, and we can keep this purely sexual. Love doesn't need to be part of this. It's not what made our chemistry great.

"I want that, too," I say on one long exhale of contained breath.

"But the risk, Jos," he says, and it's taunting. "What about the risk?"

I can't help myself. My body wants more than my mind is willing to engage in, and I rotate my hips against the hard length of him.

Kynan hisses, his hands dropping to my waist. His grip is tight, and he holds me still. "Are you going to risk it, Joslyn?"

My mind is spinning. I want him inside of me, and I have no clue what he's talking about. "Risk what?"

"Risk falling," he growls, then bites my neck again. "You know we're both on the edge. It will be so easy to tumble back again."

I blink furiously, trying to process what he's saying. Is he telling me that feelings are involved for him, too?

I pull slightly away, turning my neck so I can see him. "You're at risk?"

He doesn't answer, but his eyes bore deep into mine. "I'm a different man than I was when you knew me twelve years ago, Jos. I'm harder. Rougher. My... appetites are a bit different. You might fall into something you're not ready for."

"But what about you?" I press, needing to know this isn't a one-sided thing. "If it's just sex, let's agree on it. But if there's a chance it's more... I need to know the stakes."

Kynan's eyes close slowly, but stay that way only a moment. When they open, they're determined. "There's never been a woman like you, Joslyn. In twelve bloody years, no one's ever come close. You're fucking right I'm at risk."

Relief fills me as well as an overwhelming urgency to discover exactly what he means. A thrill of expectations rush up my spine as wetness floods my panties.

Becoming emboldened, I move my hand backward to see just *how* different, cupping his hardness through his jeans. I squeeze him roughly. Kynan groans, thrusts his hips forward, then chuckles darkly in my ear. "Do you want that?"

"Yes," I rasp. God, do I want it.

"You're going to have to work for it."

It takes a moment to process what he says, and I turn around to face him. It isn't lost on me that I have no clue how to proceed. I am the same nineteen-year-old girl who apparently hasn't led a very imaginative sex life since Kynan and I split twelve years ago.

But I do have something that has always been a part of my makeup, and I remember when there wasn't anything I wouldn't have done for this man had he asked. He definitely has something I want, and I'm willing to do what it takes to get it.

Another realization.

There's power in that as a woman.

I smile as I place my hands on his belt buckle. "Tell me what you want me to do, and I'll do it."

Fire flashes in Kynan's eyes as he bares his teeth in challenge. In a flash, he's pulling me hard into him for a kiss. His mouth covers mine. Consumes me from the inside out. One of his hands goes to the back of my head, the other to my ass to pull me flush against his hard cock.

He rips his mouth from mine, biting at my lower lip along the way. The sting of it makes me ache with need.

Rubbing a thumb roughly over my lower lip, Kynan's dark words thrill me beyond anything I could imagine. "I want something from you, Joslyn."

My chest is heaving, and it's hard to formulate words. "What's that?"

"Your mouth on me," he growls before flashing me a feral grin as he starts to take his belt off.

I want to fall to my knees right this second, because he's asking me to. I'd gladly do it. I remember the taste of him from so long ago, and I want it on my tongue again. I loved the power of having him in my mouth.

"Turn around," he orders gruffly. The hair on the nape up my neck prickles when his belt makes a hissing sound as he pulls it free from the loops.

My legs start shaking, and I can feel how embarrassingly wet I am just from what little bit of foreplay we've had—mostly from his words and dark promises.

I turn slowly away from him, staring blankly at the interior of my closet.

"Hands behind your back."

"Kynan," I murmur, not in defiance but in total supplication.

"Now, kitten," he replies with a low chuckle.

Kitten.

He used to call me that.

My hands go behind my back. Almost immediately, he's looping the thick leather of his belt around them. He cinches it tight to where I can't free myself, but there's not an ounce of pain with it.

Kynan comes around to my front. I lower my gaze automatically, instinctually submissive although I've never been tied up in my life.

"Oh, no you don't," he chides, putting his finger under my chin. He forces my eyes up to meet his. "You keep your eyes on me at all times. I promise you, Jos... you're in charge here."

I shiver.

"For now, that is," he amends.

Shivers turn into full-body shudders.

"Eyes on me," he says in reminder, then levels me with a rakish grin. "And get on your knees."

CHAPTER 19

Kynan

I'D LOVE TO be able to tell Joslyn when she wakes up it's been twelve long years since I've stayed all night in bed with a woman, but I can't.

There have been others.

Would she understand the countless women who have warmed my bed through the night were mainly due to over-consumption of alcohol? Or plain indifference? Laziness?

Would it matter?

What if I told her it has been twelve long years since I've held a woman all night? The last woman *was* Joslyn.

The night before she dumped me as a matter of fact.

There's no surge of anger or resentment. As I hold her warm body to mine, the feeling of her breath fanning across my chest divine, I can't even feel sadness for what was lost. I've always been an "in the moment" kind of man anyway.

Christ, I'm tired, which gives me the perfect excuse to just lay here and hold her. We were up all night going at each other.

And this Joslyn is a grown woman now—one who does as she pleases and takes what she wants. I like it a lot.

I was in control at first. With her hands tied behind her back, her knees pressed into the carpet, and those blue eyes pinned onto mine, I fucked her mouth. It felt better than I could have imagined, and I had to stop practically as soon as it got started. Her throat wasn't where I wanted to empty myself.

I often will fuck a woman from behind because it negates the intimacy of sex. It gives me a barrier by which I can pull totally into myself without having to look upon the beauty of a woman's face. Selfish, I know, but I'd never feel that way about Joslyn.

So when I saw the full-length mirror in that sodden big-ass closet of hers, I knew I could have the best of both words.

It was torture pulling out of her mouth and not being able to slide right home between her legs, but I'm still painfully aware of how much I hurt her the last time we were together. I hadn't even bothered getting undressed, so it was important I showed her in every action that this was different.

Sadly, I untied her hands, promising myself the belt would go back on at some point in the night. There was a lot of kissing and touching as we disrobed. She was dripping wet by the time I put her back on her knees in front of the mirror and bent her forward. When her palms hit the carpet and her fingers dug into the pile, I drove into her in one long, sweeping invasion that caused her to cry out and tighten around me.

It was the absolute best thing I'd ever felt in my life—our eyes locked through the mirror's reflection. While her face twisted and morphed through phases of pleasure, I fucked her from behind slowly and as deeply as I could. She came once, then a second time just as I had, and I thought if I died right then, my life would be complete.

I'd picked Joslyn up, carried her to the bed, and the rest of the evening was a combination of touching, whispering, talking, and fucking. Over and over again.

I shift slightly, rotating my shoulder just a bit. Joslyn's been dead weight, most of her body on mine. Stroking her hip, I relish the velvety softness of her skin. She's filled out over the years in all the right places. Gone is the lean body of youth. In its place is a gentle fullness in her curves.

Joslyn stirs. If I lay still, she could easily fall back into deep sleep, but we do have things to do today. I move my hand from her hip, slide it over an ass cheek, then I push a single finger into the valley between.

Joslyn groans and pushes against me, her voice rough with sleep. "Not again. I can't anymore."

Chuckling, I pull my hand back. Four times over the course of the night has probably left her a little sore.

Her body moves, adjusts, and I peer down. When she tilts her face, our eyes meet.

"Good morning," she says, and I hate the tentative tone.

"Morning," I reply with a smile, leaning enough so my lips can graze against her forehead.

"You stayed." There's too much wonder and awe in her statement.

"Why wouldn't I?" I tease.

She cocks a perfectly arched but highly skeptical eyebrow. "You didn't the last time."

I grin. "Touché, kitten. But truth is, you broke me last night. I didn't even have the strength to leave your bed."

For that, I get a sharp elbow in my ribs while she laughs, but then she snuggles in tighter than ever. I move from my back to my side so we're facing each other, wrapping both arms around her. Our faces are so close it makes staring difficult as she goes all blurry around the edges.

"Last night was intense," she murmurs.

Loosening my hold, I put enough distance between us that I can focus on her face. Her cheeks are pink, hair all messy and tangled. She looks like she got fucked four times last night... and not once was she held back upon.

"Which part?" I ask, curious as to what stands out in her mind the most.

"All of it," she admits, bringing a fingertip up to trace my collarbone. "So different than how we used to be."

"We're different people, Jos."

"I suppose," she murmurs thoughtfully, her gaze now going to her finger that has started to trace patterns on my chest.

When she doesn't say anymore, I push a bit. "You've become an adventurous woman, kitten. You took everything I gave you. Hell, half the time you were begging me for more."

Joslyn snorts, eyes sparkling with amusement. "Half the time, you didn't give me a choice as to what I would or wouldn't take. You just did what you wanted."

"And you loved it," I assert boldly.

She doesn't deny it, merely lets her lips tip upward in a very private smile that only she understands the meaning of. But I think I am starting to.

"Tell me about that sex club you were going to," she asks out of the blue.

I blink a moment. "Pardon?"

"When I went to your house last week in Vegas." She looks me dead in the eye, not a trace of jealousy in her tone, only curiosity. "You were with that woman. You said you met her in a sex club."

"The Wicked Horse," I murmur, stunned she's asking me about it.

"What's it like?" Her eyes are wide, her voice filled with awe, and I think some of the things I did to her last night have her wondering.

"It's absolute freedom," I state, not doubting the first words that come to mind. "It's an environment where you can push all your limits with likeminded people."

"You couldn't be more vague if you tried," she censures.

"What do you want to know?" I ask, not sure I really want to reveal anything about The Wicked Horse. For the last three years, I've been a member there and I have done nothing but enjoy it to the utmost. It's been my escape several nights a week—a place where I can let go of everything.

And yet... here I find myself fearful Joslyn will disapprove if she knows more about it.

"Well," she drawls as her forehead scrunches in consideration. "I mean... like do you go there and sleep with a different person each time?"

"Most of the time." I shrug. "Sometimes, I'll be with a person more than once."

"And you just... have sex in front of others?"

"Always. There's no privacy there."

"It's what? A big orgy?" She blinks with wide, curious eyes. "Are you friends with the people there? Do you have long-term relationships—"

I put my hand to her jaw and grip it lightly, but firmly so she can't look away. "It's a place I went to, Joslyn, because it allowed me to have release without any commitment. It wasn't necessary for my pleasure or happiness, yet I did enjoy my times there. I'll never lie about that."

"Will you miss it when you move to Pittsburgh?" she asks, and that sets me back as I have to think about that.

And I determine... no. I won't miss it.

I'll miss *this*, though. Lying next to her all night. Having ridiculous conversations in the morning.

"No, I won't miss it."

She opens her mouth, another burning question to ask, but I'm saved by my phone ringing. The high-powered notes of Heart's "Barracuda" cut over her and I smile. "That's Rachel. I better get it."

Reluctantly, I let Joslyn go and roll toward the nightstand. I'd fished my phone out of my discarded jeans in her closet at some point in the night and put it within reach. I nab it, connect the call, and roll toward Joslyn as I say to Rachel, "What's up?"

I catch sight of Joslyn's beautifully perfect ass—that I'd done very naughty things to last night—as she attempts to roll out of bed. My arm shoots out, wraps around her middle, and I haul her into me. "I'm not quite finished with you."

"Finished with me what?" Rachel asks through the phone line.

"Nothing," I reply with a smirk as Joslyn settles into me with no argument as I come to my side. She wiggles that luscious ass, and my dick instantly responds. "I'm talking to Joslyn. So the call better be important."

Joslyn snickers, and Rachel does the same thing before saying, "It's important. Just wanted to let you know, Bebe checked all the city street cameras around the flower shop to see if she could follow our stalker to his car and perhaps get a license plate number."

I have a moment of intense pride for Bebe and her criminality, as well as her fearlessness in breaking the rules. It's exactly what I want from her. I go ahead and put the phone on speaker so Joslyn can listen in. She shifts in my arms, then flips to her back so she can see me. "What did she find?"

"Sadly, nothing so far," Rachel says with a sigh. "She was able to follow him for a few blocks, but he parked his car down a side alley."

"Shit," I mutter.

"She checked the back entrances for the businesses there. One had a security camera, but it wasn't working."

Double shit.

"And get this," Rachel continues. "She hacked the camera on the other side of the block that would point toward the other end of the one-way alley where he'd parked."

"But it was broken, too," I hazard a guess.

"Actually, no... it was working. But it was turned off for a very defined period of time. From about half an hour before the guy pulled his car into the alley until about an hour after he left."

"So for an hour and a half, the camera facing the alley where the stalker parked was turned off," I repeat thoughtfully. "Coincidence?"

"I doubt it," she replies. I don't believe in coincidence either, so I concur.

"We have a guy who is sophisticated enough to cover any tracks that could lead to his identification."

"With special emphasis in hacking," Rachel adds. "He's got to have skills to breach the city's database. Bebe's not giving up, though. She's actually going to broaden the search. She's going to access footage of nearby cameras and the vehicles that go by."

"That's pretty labor intensive," I remark.

"We've got nothing better to do," Rachel replies with a knowing chuckle. "And before I forget... everything is set for Bebe next week."

"She have any clue?" I ask.

"None," Rachel assures me. "It will be epic."

"Yes, it will. Now, I've got better things to do than chitchat with you, so if you don't mind—"

"Later, boss," Rachel chirps before hanging up the

phone.

Tossing mine over my shoulder, I give Joslyn a lascivious smile. "Now," I drawl as I bring my hand to her belly and start to slide it downward. "I passionately believe you should start every day with a mind-blowing orgasm. But since you were a good girl last night, I'll give you two."

Joslyn's hand latches onto my wrist just before my fingers reach her promised land and halt my progress. With her eyebrows drawn inward and her tone clipped, she asks, "What were you talking about when you asked Rachel if Bebe has any clue? Any clue about what?"

Christ, she's adorable, coming to Bebe's defense without even really knowing if she's in trouble. All Joslyn heard was Rachel and I are hiding something, and now she's ready to go all hell-cat on us. More importantly, she means to deny my fingers entrance to her slick heat.

"Relax, kitten, and sheath those claws," I tease her in a gruff voice. I easily break her hold, then slide a long finger inside of her. Her hips shoot upward, and she groans. "I just arranged for Bebe's mom and son to fly to Vegas to surprise her."

Joslyn's hand slaps onto my wrist, holding me tight in place. I could move if I wanted to, but by the expression on her face, I'm powerless to do anything but stare.

She's giving me a look of such utter respect and tenderness, it makes my chest feel like it's on fire while, oddly, making my dick harder than ever. I realize... I want to see that look from her every day, wondering what I'd have to give a woman like her just for a single momentary glimpse of it.

Joslyn lays her palm on my cheek. Her thumb grazes it gently. "You are an incredible man, Kynan."

It's more than I need to hear, and I'm not ready to confront the emotions her praise pulls forth. So I pull my finger out, add another, and start to pump. Joslyn's eyes glaze over, expression morphing into a woman lost to the pleasure I can give her.

And that's enough for right now.

CHAPTER 20

Joslyn

"WHAT ELSE DO you want?" I ask Kynan as I lean over the island counter. I had just scribbled down "Cherry Garcia ice cream" on my shopping list.

Kynan stares at his laptop on the opposite side. He's perched there, looking incredibly yummy in just a tank top and workout shorts. We plan on hitting the gym first, then we're going grocery shopping.

Sort of like a couple, but not. He's my bodyguard. But like a couple because he's been very vocal about what items he wants.

"Add some Smithwick's, will you, love?" he asks, and I grin as I write down his request.

It's weird how we've settled into this oddly natural routine with each other the past three days since we... became intimate again.

And intimate is exactly the word I'd use to describe the nature of our relationship now. Because what he did to me in that closet was equal parts lewd, erotic, and debasing. It was the most intimate connection I've ever had with another human being in my entire life.

When he was behind me—in me—and we stared at each other in the mirror, not once breaking that connection until it was over, I realized Kynan is the only man I could hope to have that with. Our bond was forged twelve years ago, and I had once thought it was broken.

It isn't.

It was only put on ice. Now, it's been thawed and has since heated to nuclear proportions.

Kynan and I have gone out to dinner each night. Somewhere swank, always where the paparazzi hang out. I'm trending under the hashtag #celebritycouples, and tongues are wagging about my quick and totally romantic engagement to my first true love. Of course... I've been wearing the sapphire ring whenever we go out—to lend credence to the story.

In public, Kynan is doting, romantic, and affectionate.

Privately, he is doting, romantic, and affectionate. It is no hardship for me to return the same to him. The animosity between us has simply faded.

The nights are indescribable. He makes me feel things I've never felt before. Does things to my body I didn't know were possible. He's been inside places I didn't think I'd ever let a man, yet I find I crave him everywhere. Anywhere.

Last night, he pressed a long finger inside my back-side while he was fucking me, and I orgasmed immediately from the shock of it. Laughing darkly, he'd said he was going to fuck me back there one day. I was immediately turned on, horrified, and scared at the same time. But when he wants to do that, I'm going to let him.

"Anything else you want me to add?" I ask one last time, while I scratch the word "lube" on my list. Why not?

"No, that's all," he says. Closing his laptop, he smiles, and it reaches my heart. "Ready to go?"

"In a minute. I want to check my email first."

"Okay," he says, continuing to watch me as I move from behind the island. I walk into the great room, glance over my shoulder, and find Kynan still continuing to watch me.

"What?" I ask with a laugh. "Why are you staring?"

"Because I like it," he replies cheekily.

When I roll my eyes, his smile fades as his eyes glint dangerously.

"Did you just roll your eyes?" he asks darkly.

"What if I did?" I ask, swiveling to fully face him with a hand on my hip.

"If you did," he drawls while slowly standing from the kitchen stool. "I might just have to redden that ass."

I'll never admit that every fiber in my being would

like that. He spanked me the other night in between using my vibrator on me, and I lost count of how many times I came. Still, I shake my head. "We don't have time. We have to get to the gym, the grocery store, dry cleaners, and then come back so I can start getting dinner ready for—"

That's as far as I get before Kynan lunges. I manage a half shriek before he's lifted and thrown me across his shoulder, only to take two steps to the nearest couch where he tosses me down.

Half an hour later, my ass is on fire and I have a smile on my face.

◆

THERE'S A BOX sitting on my front porch when we pull into the driveway. I don't say a word, but perhaps Kynan saw me imperceptibly tighten up or he just got a vibe from me, but he's quick to reassure me. "That's something I ordered."

"How do you know?" I ask.

"Because I have an app on my phone that alerts me when the cameras are triggered, so I saw the UPS man deliver it. Plus, I was expecting it."

"What is it?"

"You'll see," he says, turning the car off.

Kynan insists on carrying all the grocery bags in the house, which is fine. My arms are noodles after our workout. Kynan is in impeccable shape, while I realized I need to work out a lot more consistently. I'm going to be sore tomorrow, which means I should probably schedule a massage. I have a meeting tomorrow with a producer who is doing a movie about the legendary Dolly Parton and wants to discuss my interest in the role.

Although, "lack of interest" might be the better term. I was given the script a few weeks ago, and I passed on it. Making movies isn't my thing. Frankly, I'm not sure I can pull Dolly off. She's the queen. Legendary. I'm just... Joslyn Meyers.

I follow Kynan into the kitchen. After he deposits the bags, I start going through them, putting things where they belong. He disappears, then returns with the cardboard box in his hand.

"I had Rachel and Bebe working on a little project for me," Kynan announces as he rummages in the drawer for a steak knife.

He finds one, then deftly slices through the tape. From within, he pulls out a small box. I pause, stunned when a pair of silver earrings are revealed. "What are those?"

"Earrings, kitten," he replies with a smile.

I start to roll my eyes—but stop upon realizing it will only sidetrack us further—and ask, "I can see that. But what are they for?"

"For you." He walks around the counter and approaches me, holding the jewelry out in the palm of his hand.

I have to admit—they're totally my style. A little funky and bohemian. Puffed silver squares with scrolled etchings in the metal that hang from a simple hook. I pick them up, surprised at how incredibly light they are.

"Put them in," Kynan orders me. "And only take them out to sleep. Otherwise, they stay in at all times."

"Why?" I put them on the counter for a moment so I can remove the tiny gold hoops in my ears.

"Bebe fit them with a tracking device."

"Why would you need to track me?" I ask as I put the first one in.

Kynan's eyes turn cold and hard. "God help me. I don't even want to imagine it, but if for some reason that bastard was able to get his hands on you, I wanted a tertiary plan to be able to find you."

"Tertiary? That's the third plan. What's the first and second?" The other earring slides right in. They're so light I can't feel them, and I'm immediately impressed with the technology.

"First is he doesn't get his hands on you," Kynan growls before pulling another small box from the package. "If he does manage to get past me, I've got trackers for your phone and for the inside lining of your purse. This guy is smart, though, and I imagine he wouldn't let you keep those for long."

And it suddenly hits me. While I trust Kynan implicitly, it's become clear he's not infallible. If my stalker gets me, it would mean Kynan was probably... dead.

"Whoa there," Kynan exclaims as my legs turn to jelly. He steps in to wrap his arms around my waist before I fall. "Got a little pale there, Jos."

I put my hands on his shoulders, my voice laced with a panic I can't seem to quell. "You're implying if he gets me, something terrible has happened to you. I can't live with that, Kynan."

"Nothing's going to happen to me, love," he murmurs, dipping just a bit to put his face right in front of mine. "I promise."

"Then I don't need these backup plans, right?" The hysteria seems to be rising as this question comes out sort of like a screech.

Kynan smiles before pressing his mouth to mine. When he pulls back, he looks me right in the eye. "I am ninety-nine percent positive nothing is going to happen to me or you. But hypothetically, let's just say I was to have a brain aneurysm at the same exact time this guy tried to make a move. In that extremely specific instance, I want a backup plan as well as a backup plan to that plan, okay?"

"It's not funny," I grouse, trying to push him away. "It just suddenly hit me... you're in as much danger as I am. I mean, he could be waiting in the bushes for me and have a gun. He could shoot you or something."

"Joslyn," he says softly, but the soothing tone isn't working. I feel dizzy. "Take a deep breath, love. Nice deep breath."

I do so, letting it out slowly.

"Again," he urges me.

My lungs expand as I draw in a breath, hold it a moment with my eyes closed, then let it out again.

When I open my eyes, Kynan's face is all I see. It's awash with empathy.

"I'm sorry," I murmur. "I don't want to be a baby about all this. I just... it never hit me that we might not win, and—"

"We're going to bloody well win," Kynan growls. "I swear to fuck, Joslyn. I won't ever let anything bad happen to you."

My breath rushes out, some I'd been holding onto deep in my chest. I manage a smile, although it doesn't really match how I feel on the inside. I even nod in agreement, because I don't want him worrying about me.

I let myself lean forward—fall really—into his chest, and I take comfort in the way he wraps his arms around me. In protection. "I know. I trust you."

I revel in the security only for a moment. Truly not wanting him to worry, I pull away and give him a confident smile. "I'm going to go grab a shower before I start dinner."

"I could join you in the shower," he suggests with a leering grin, his hands dropping to my hips to hold me in place. "Then help you with dinner."

I like this idea a lot. Despite knowing this man for over twelve years and being intimate with him on countless occasions, we have never taken a shower or a bath together. My smile turns brighter. "Deal. I'm just going to check my email first. I got sidetracked earlier when you insisted on reddening my ass. Mom was going to send me a recipe I want to try tonight."

"I'll go get the shower running," he says, giving a light slap to said ass. "Don't keep me waiting."

"Wouldn't dream of it," I reply dryly.

Kynan heads to the master suite, and I go to my office. It takes only a second for me to pull my laptop out of sleep mode and open up Gmail.

Mom's email is at the top, the subject line reading "Apple Hickory Pork Loin".

"Perfect," I murmur, moving the cursor to open it so I can print the recipe, but something catches my eye.

It's the email right below.

The subject line says, "Naughty Girl".

I focus on the sender. The email address is nondescript, and I don't recognize it—*waxon42@gmail.com*

It's the "Naughty Girl" that has my blood turning cold. My hand shakes as I slide my finger over the track pad and double click to open the email.

I quickly scan over the words, and nausea rises within me.

> *You've been a very naughty girl, Joslyn. Actually hiring someone to try to thwart me. But don't worry. I'm not mad about that—more like amused.*
>
> *What pisses me off is you think you belong to anyone but me.*
>
> *You are mine.*
>
> *And when I finally have you, I'm going to make you pay for letting another man touch you.*
>
> *Until we meet again…*

He's coming. This is proof positive he'd taken the bait. It had pissed him off just as Kynan said it would.

I should feel relieved. Instead, I'm terrified.

"Kynan," I call, raising my voice loud enough he should be able to hear it above the sound of the shower. Then I up the volume just a little more. "*Kynan.*"

CHAPTER 21

Kynan

"TELL ME YOU can find the fucker," I growl as I pace the interior of Joslyn's office with my phone in hand. She's sitting in her desk chair, eyes glued on me.

Bebe's voice comes to me over the speaker on my phone. She's remote accessed Joslyn's computer to see the email from the Jameson offices in Vegas. "I'll try, but I doubt I'll have any luck. This guy has major skills. I'm sure he's used a VPN or even the dark web to obscure his location."

Not good enough. "Bloody hell, Bebe. I sprung you from prison. You've got to give me more than 'I can try'."

Joslyn's eyes flare wide, because my tone is almost threatening in nature. Sighing, I prepare to apologize, but Bebe doesn't seem fazed. Her voice is bland. "I can only do so much with the laptop you bought me, Kynan. You want me to locate this guy, then it's going to take equipment you can't buy on the open market."

That gets my attention. "But there is a way if I got

you the right stuff?"

"Yeah, sure," she replies. "It's all black-market stuff, which I'm sensing doesn't matter to you. But it will take time, and I'm betting we don't have that."

"Fuck," I mutter, scrubbing my hand through my hair in agitation. Joslyn stands from her chair. "Where are you going?"

"I'm going to start dinner," she replies softly. "You don't need me involved in this."

"Hold on, Bebe," I say, then tap the "mute" button. Moving to Joslyn, I put my hand on her shoulder.

Dipping my head, I put my eyes level with hers. "You okay?"

Her smile is wan, but it doesn't appear to be forced. "I'm fine. You're doing your thing with Bebe, and you don't need me in here for that. I'm better off staying busy, so I'll go start dinner."

It's hard for me to understand how just five minutes ago, I was turning on the shower in Joslyn's master bath with about a million dirty thoughts in my head. Then her scream almost had my heart exploding. When I read that fucker's email, I almost stroked out.

It's what I'd wanted to happen. I wanted to goad him into action, but now I have his undivided attention, I'm feeling a little unsure of just how prepared I am. Bebe not being able to wave a magic wand to find this guy by his email isn't something I want to really hear right now.

What I want is this guy's address so I can track him down, probably beat him with my bare hands until he's a bloody mess, and then haul him off to the police station.

I pull Joslyn toward me, brush my mouth against hers, and murmur, "Don't start dinner. We're going out instead, so go ahead and hit the shower."

"We are?"

"Yeah. If this guy is watching you closely as I suspect, I don't want him to think this has you rattled in any way. I want him to see you strong, and he's totally going to see us as a unit."

Joslyn sighs. She's a little tired of all the hobnobbing and socializing we've done the last few days as we've splashed ourselves around the celebrity circuit. We had both been looking forward to a quiet evening in.

But now her stalker is good and pissed, and I want to throw it in his face she's not scared. We're not intimidated.

And if I'm lucky, he might make a move in public. I've got security on her house so tight the chances of him trying to attack her on this turf is unlikely. Him finding her on her own is more than unlikely because Joslyn's not going anywhere outside this house without me or a suitable alternative.

"Go on," I urge, relieved when she goes to her tiptoes to put a kiss on my lips. It's soft and lingering without a hint of sex, but it speaks volumes to me. She turns without another word, leaving her office.

When she's disappeared, I reconnect the call to Bebe. "I'm back. Listen… do the best you can. When you get a free moment, I want you to compile your dream list of equipment along with a rough estimate of the cost. And when I say dream list, I'm not just talking about for the stuff we're doing now. Anything you can imagine that would give you access to anything we could ever dream of doing. Do you understand?"

"As long as you're not going to ask me to use this stuff for evil," Bebe drawls, and it makes me laugh.

"Do the best you can right now with what you have. Push whatever boundaries you need to. I've got your back."

"I know you do," she replies, and it occurs to me that she's put a lot of trust in me in a truly short amount of time. She's either a really good judge of character or she knows she's got nothing left to lose. "Also… if you have contacts with the FBI as I suspect you do, they have the means to track this type of thing to an exact location. Of course, it doesn't necessarily mean it's going to be where this guy is living or anything. But if you have a favor owed there, I'd collect on it."

"When we hang up, tell Rachel to call Ted Griss," I reply because it just so happens, I do. "He owes me a couple of favors, and she'll get him working on this."

"One more thing." Her tone is hesitant, almost as if she had to work up the guts to tell me something. "I have an idea that might be able to lead us to him if he continues to send her stuff through the internet."

"What's that?"

"I was thinking... maybe I could lay a trap for him. Let him hack his way in for some information, then I can lay some code that will reverse track him."

"But can't he circumvent like you said before... with VPN or something?"

"Yes, but I'd plant a sort of virus that will attach itself to him, and well... so as not to get technical, it would be like leaving me a trail of bread crumbs to follow back to him, so to speak."

"You can do that?" I ask.

"I don't know. It's really just theory."

"What's the risk? Downside?"

"He sees it," she replies cautiously. "Reverse hacks me. Jameson. I mean, I don't know his level of expertise, but it isn't without risk. We could be poking a very smart bear."

I consider this, not wanting to put Jameson at risk. While I have a lot of confidence in Bebe's abilities, I'm not technical enough to know just how serious these risks are.

"I'm pretty sure I can hide my tracks," she says. "But I can't guarantee it."

"Let me think about it." It ultimately may be moot because if this guy is ready to make a move, it will probably be sooner rather than later. "Just do what you can right now with what we've discussed."

"Got it. Later, boss," she replies and disconnects. I like that about her. She doesn't waste time.

I immediately flip through my contacts on my phone, then select Cruce Britton from the list.

It was eight days ago I interviewed him.

Seven days ago, he talked to a U.S. Senator and the director of the Defense Intelligence Agency, both of whom gave stellar references for me and my company. I also offered my mum's phone number if he wanted to talk to her for a personal reference, but he declined.

Six days ago, he accepted my offer of employment. Of course, I wasn't ready for him to start right away as I was dealing with this shitbag of a stalker, but I figured the signing bonus I gave him more than made up for the delay.

But now... I'm ready for him to start.

I tap on his contact, and he answers on the second ring by saying my first name. "Kynan."

"I need you out here in Santa Barbara," I say. I had filled him in briefly on Joslyn's case when we last spoke, so it won't take him long to get up to speed.

"I'll book the next flight out," he says.

"No. Head to the airport. I'll charter a jet for you to

leave tomorrow morning."

"Weapons?" is his only question.

"Load up," I reply and disconnect.

Tapping my phone against my chin, I take a moment to think if there's anything else I need to do. Before Bebe got on the phone, I had spoken to Rachel briefly. She's going to call the lead detective who was working the case to update him with everything that's occurred, but I'm not counting on them to do much. Maybe increased patrols around Joslyn's home, but there's just not much they can do.

I've done all I can in this moment. Probably until we either get a break on identifying this sodden scum or he makes a move. Until then, the waiting game is the only one I can play.

I move to Joslyn's room, the sound of the hissing shower leading me to her. I start removing my clothes in the hallway. By the time I hit the bathroom, I'm naked. I can see her through the opaque glass door to her shower, standing with her head bowed so the water can hit her between the shoulder blades.

She looks small and defeated, and my protective instincts kick in. It has nothing to do with the job I've been hired to perform, but it has everything to do with needing her safe and secure so I can keep her in my life.

When I pull the door open, she raises her head. Water streams down her face, catches in her lashes, and leaves droplets on her lips. She's never looked more desirable to me, and I need nothing from her right now other than her trust that I will take care of everything.

I open my arms, and there's no hesitation before her body moves into mine. Joslyn's cheek goes to my chest, and we wrap our arms around each other. "I won't let him near you, kitten. I promise you are safe, okay?"

She squeezes me. "I know. I trust you."

"Bebe's working on tracking him, but it's a long shot. I've also asked Cruce to come out here as backup."

She jolts and pulls her head back in question.

"I just want the backup, Jos," I explain. "You're too important, and I'm just not willing to leave anything up to chance."

"Okay," she replies with a nod. "I understand."

"Do you? Understand?" I ask, not able to hide the urgency in my tone. "This is more than just a job to me."

Her large blue eyes just blink as she stares.

"*You* are more than just a job to me," I clarify.

I need her to know that. I need her to know there is no resentment left for what was done to us. I sure as fuck don't know what the future holds, but I do know she holds some place in it.

Joslyn responds by winding her arms around my neck, then pulling my mouth down to hers. She kisses me sweetly at first, but then it turns sensual as her tongue slips in my mouth and her body melds into mine. I force every bit of worry, planning, and strategy out of my head, and I concentrate on this amazing woman in my arms.

The woman I once loved with all my heart—who I'm fairly certain I've fallen right back in love with. Thus, keeping her safe and taking this stalker down just became the most important thing I'll ever do in my life because I'm ready to see what waits on the other side of that for Joslyn and me.

CHAPTER 22

Joslyn

IT'S ONLY A fifteen-minute drive from my house to the airport in Santa Barbara to pick up Cruce, but just getting out for even a bit is nice.

It's not that we don't go out because we do. We go out in splashy fashion to make sure I end up on as many TV and social media feeds as possible. All part of the plan to piss my stalker off.

But that type of event is exhausting. I have to go full hair, makeup, and designer clothing. Cameras are in our face, and it's hard to just be ourselves.

This short trip to the airport, though, is exactly what I needed. I've got my hair in a ponytail and under a ball cap with nothing on my face except some mascara. I'm rocking a pair of faded jeans, a flowing, pale yellow bohemian blouse, and my flip-flops. Kynan is just as casual. Jeans and a t-shirt that fit very, very well. He's also got a cap on his head, a pair of sunglasses, and just the right amount of stubble on his face. He's the most gorgeous man I've ever known in my life, and everything about him pushes my buttons.

"Nice smile you got going there," Kynan says, and I hadn't realized he'd even seen. He's driving after all.

My teeth flash, grin getting broader. "This is such a free moment out of the house with no agenda. I'm feeling incredibly happy right now."

"I like you being happy," he replies, reaching over and taking my hand. He laces his fingers with mine, and we rest our arms on the center console. "I also think it's good your mom is coming to visit. You could use some quality downtime with her."

"Agreed," I answer as I watch the scenery fly by. "I'm really looking forward to it."

My mom has been in close contact with me since we left her house almost a full week ago. She's incredibly worried about me and my stalker situation, but she's also hell-bent on furthering amends by inviting herself and Darren for a visit.

It's not necessary, though—her needing to make things right with me. I know she's sorry for what she did, but I'm also not going to keep her at arm's length either. I've been longing for my relationship with her to get back to what I remember before I became a celebrity.

The only thing I don't like is Kynan feels it's best if they stay at a hotel rather than the house. He said this was for security reasons, and I have to trust him. Kynan explained more people in the house meant he was accountable for more than just my safety. He personally wanted to focus everything on me, and I understand this. Moreover, once he told my mom and Darren, they totally understood. Instead, I booked them a room at the Four Seasons. We'll spend quality time together, but she and Darren will stay there at night.

"This is a nice area," Kynan remarks as he glances out my window at the Santa Ynez mountains to the west.

"It's called the American Riviera."

"Is that why there are so many red-tiled roofs?"

I laugh. "I think it's more because our climate is more in tune with the Mediterranean. But I do love it here. I thought maybe I'd be safer moving away from the Los Angeles area, but apparently not. Still, the slower pace speaks to me at this point in my life."

"What do you mean?"

I twist slightly in my seat toward him. His fingers tighten on mine, so our hold doesn't break. "I was just getting to a point in my career I wanted to slow down."

"You? Slow down?" he teases.

I toss my head back and laugh, because I am a little hard to hold down at times. But when it wanes and there's only a slight chuckle left, I explain. "I'm just tired of it all. The pace. The work. The spotlight."

"You're too young to retire," he points out. That's totally true as I'd never be able to sit still, and he knows that about me.

"I know, even though I have enough money I'd never have to work another day in my life, I guess I just want to do something that fills my well, so to speak. I want to find my joy and passion again."

"Singing and acting doesn't make you happy?"

I give a mirthless laugh. "Of course it does. But it's also such a lonely career. You never really have close friends, and someone is always trying to get something out of you. I mean... look at my mom. My career became more important to her than anything."

"Fame has a way of fucking with people," he replies sagely. "But not you... you stayed humble and genuine."

"Regardless, I've sort of got a fresh perspective now, so I've been thinking about it a lot more."

"Fresh perspective? A man breaking into your house and attacking you?"

"Well that," I reply sardonically. "But also... reuniting with you."

I get a squeeze to my hand, and a dimple pops in the corner of his cheek as he smiles. "If you could pick one thing to do for the rest of your life, what would it be?" Kynan ever wanting to boil down to simplicities. He's amazing at focusing in on the important things.

"Song writing," I reply with no hesitation. "That's where I get the most joy—writing the songs and in the music."

"I can see that," he says with a slow nod. "I remember when you used to come off stage in Vegas and you'd just sag into Michel's waiting arms as the adrenaline deserted you. While I know you were great at performing and you had some fun at it, I never felt the reward was enough to overcome the stress of it all."

"And yet I've managed to make a career of it," I point out.

"So make a new career," he says. "Like you said, it's not like you need the money. You should write songs and be happy."

"But what if I miss performing? Or acting?" Because it's never simple for me. I'd always wonder if I was making a mistake by walking away at the height of my career.

"I'm pretty sure there will be a spot waiting for you if you want to go back to it," he replies dryly, making his point. I'm letting silly things hold me back. "If you changed your career path, what are some other things you'd want to do?"

"Oh, I don't know," I hedge, staring out the passenger window.

"Don't play coy, Joslyn Meyers," Kynan reprimands. "You are a woman who always thinks ahead."

I snort and then turn back. "The usual. Develop a hobby or two. Take time to smell the roses. A dog. Kids."

Kynan's eyebrows shoot up. "Kids? How many?"

I shrug. "One. Two. Definitely no more than two."

Releasing my hand, Kynan scrubs his own over his short beard and gives me another quick glance before giving his attention back to the road. "You and I have been having unprotected sex. That's not been very smart of us."

"Tell me about it," I say with a snort as I lean back into my seat, giving him a haughty sneer down my nose. "And you go to a sex club. What was I thinking?"

"Bollocks," Kynan says a little sharply. "I would never put you at risk. I always used a condom. Always. You're the only woman I've ever not used protection with."

Laughing, I pat him on the arm. "I was just teasing you, Kynan. I know you wouldn't put me at risk. And I'm assuming you know the same about me."

"Yeah," he says with a long sigh. "I know that. But you mentioned kids and that got me thinking that—"

"I'm on birth control," I cut in. "I get the shot so it's not something you have to worry about."

"I'm not worried, Jos," he says solemnly as we approach the private air terminal where Cruce is flying in. Kynan paid a private charter jet so he could bring weapons, which both scares and relieves me.

Up ahead, standing outside the terminal is the man I recognize as Cruce Britton. I had seen him when he came to interview with Kynan at the new Jameson headquarters, but we had not been introduced. He's dressed in jeans and a pullover. He's got a small suitcase on the ground along with an olive-green military-sized duffel I'm betting is chock-full of goodies.

As Kynan slows the vehicle, another thought occurs that has nothing to do with Cruce. "Why didn't you use a condom with me?"

Not seeming fazed by my question, he brings the car to a smooth stop beside Cruce, who is on the passenger side. Kynan leans over the console, dipping down so he can see Cruce outside my window. Kynan holds up just one finger, indicating he needs just a moment.

Then he tilts until he's face-to-face with me. "I didn't wear a condom because I didn't want a bloody thing between us."

"Oh," I say quietly, a little in awe that was the case since he was terribly angry with me then.

"And since then," he goes on to say in a low, deep voice that does funny things to the area between my legs, "I've kept doing it because it feels too fucking good. It's primal, Jos. I love coming inside of you. Call me a caveman or what have you, but I love marking the inside of you with me."

My jaw drops, and I am at a complete loss for words. All I want in this moment is to pull him in the backseat with me and have him mark me right now.

This very moment.

Instead, he grins before plastering a hard, quick kiss to my mouth. What Cruce is thinking of this, I have no clue, but then Kynan is pressing the button to release the trunk and Cruce is there loading his duffel and suitcase.

Kynan leans back fully into his seat, merely glancing over his shoulder at Cruce as he slides into the backseat. "Thanks for coming, man."

"My pleasure," Cruce replies as he closes the door.

Kynan makes a quick introduction. "Cruce. Joslyn."

I twist in my seat, Cruce leans forward, and we manage a quick handshake. I smile and say, "Welcome to Santa Barbara."

"Know the area well," he replies as he settles back and puts on his seatbelt. Kynan pulls away from the curb as Cruce continues. "I worked the L.A. investigative office when I first joined the Secret Service, but I spent a lot of downtime up this way."

We chitchat some more, and I find Cruce to be affable and outgoing. He doesn't have that overriding serious nature Kynan bears much of the time, but I can also tell if Cruce were to get serious about something, he'd be a force. Kynan had told me about who he really was... the man credited with saving then vice president's—now president—life. Of course I knew that story, but I never would have connected his name to the incident.

It's comforting knowing I've got him on our side until this thing is resolved.

Kynan eventually commandeers the conversation, turning to business. He gives Cruce the low down on my security system and what we've learned about the stalker—including his scary brilliant hacking abilities. The men start brainstorming, and I recline and just listen. My few minutes of a carefree day are over, and it's back to reality.

CHAPTER 23

Kynan

CRUCE AND I walk the rear of Joslyn's property, which has a thick border of laurel and scrub oak. It's a good place for a creeper to hide and watch her house from a distance, so I check it often. I've also installed wireless cameras in a few of the trees, hidden on a secured network Bebe monitors with alarm measures to ensure they're not hacked. So far, it doesn't appear Joslyn's stalker has tried to breach her property since he left the sunflowers, but I am expecting him to make a move any day. I've even thought about having Bebe let him into the system if he tries, to see if we can lure him into some complacency.

It's hard to know what to do, though. Joslyn isn't the first person I've protected from something such as this, but the stakes have never been so personally high. My frustration in not knowing who we're dealing with is starting to take a toll. If this doesn't end soon, there's no telling what I'm doing to do to this bastard when we finally get him.

"Joslyn wants to have breakfast with her mom tomorrow morning, then go out and do some shopping," I tell Cruce as we stroll. It looks like a relaxed meander to the casual observer, but we've both got our eyes peeled sharply for any bit of evidence to indicate her stalker has been here or for a potential weakness in our defense.

"Want me to take them?" he guesses.

"Yeah, and only because I'm going to interview another potential candidate for Jameson," I reply. "He's in California on business, so he's going to stop by here."

"Anyone I know?" Cruce asks curiously.

"Not unless international theft is your gig," I answer with a laugh.

Chuckling, he shakes his head. "Not my scene, but he sounds interesting."

"Trust me," I drawl as we turn toward the house. "Saint Bellinger is quite the character."

"Well, then I look forward to meeting him if he makes your cut." We move through the middle of the yard and walk toward the pool. I've yet to see Joslyn use it despite the fact it's heated and the weather has been nice. Cruce stops at the edge. "If you're doing some active recruiting, I've got someone you might be interested in."

"Oh yeah?"

Cruce nods. "His name is Malik Fournier. He's finishing up an enlistment in the U.S. Marine Corps now.

2D Recon."

"I'm always interested in someone with a Special Forces background. Solid guy?"

"The best," Cruce replies. "He did a temporary detail at the White House and got to know the president pretty well. His brothers are professional hockey players. Lucas and Max Fournier, who play for Carolina Cold Fury."

Shrugging, I shake my head. "Sorry, mate. I'm a football kind of guy... and by football for you Yanks, I mean soccer."

Cruce laughs. "If you want to talk to him, I'll give him a call."

"Do that," I say head before heading toward the back door. "I'm going to go check on Joslyn."

"I'll make another sweep of the perimeter," Cruce says.

I throw a hand up, calling over my shoulder. "Joslyn's going to make dinner tonight. Figure we'll eat around seven or so."

"Roger that," he replies, then I put Cruce out of my mind. He's been a good houseguest the last two days. Unobtrusive, yet he always has his eye on Joslyn the same as I do. I feel better having him here.

I enter through the patio door that leads into the great room. The alarm chimes since we leave it engaged at all times, and I enter the code into my phone app rather than the keypad on the wall. Just a habit. It's amazing how much shit can be utilized through a phone these days.

It's getting close to dusk. When I'd left Joslyn about half an hour ago, she was in her room reading a book. She's got a window nook with a padded bench and fluffy pillows, and she seemed happy and content just relaxing, although I know appearances can be deceiving.

Joslyn is asleep when I walk into her room. Head nestled on a pillow, legs curled under her, and her book face down on her chest.

Smiling, I move to sit on the edge of the padded bench near her hip. My eyes drop to the book. There's a bare-chested dude—amazingly built—on the cover.

I pick the book up for a closer inspection. Apparently, Joslyn wasn't sleeping deeply as she immediately rouses.

"Hey," she says in a raspy voice as she rubs her eyes.

Cocking an eyebrow, I hold the book up. "Just what is this?"

"It's a romance book," she snaps, but her lips curve up. She snatches it from my hand, then tucks it behind her back. "You should read it. Bet you could learn a thing or two, McGrath."

I give an offended grunt, shooting her a stern look. "There's nothing in those books I can't do a million times better."

"What makes you think they do anything at all?" she quips, eyes sparkling with amusement.

"Based on the cover, as a consumer, I'd have to expect he has to do something other than flexing his muscles."

Joslyn laughs and pulls her legs up, wrapping her hands around her shins. She grins. "As a matter of fact, you're a lot like some of the men in these books. Bossy, alpha, overprotective, and extremely great in bed."

"I am not bossy," I growl with mock offense.

"A little." She holds her hand up, forefinger and thumb about an inch apart.

"I am great in bed, though," I admit as I puff my chest out. "In case you've forgotten, I'll prove it to you again tonight."

Joslyn rolls her eyes, knowing it puts her ass in danger of connecting with the palm of my hand. But it's too cute to call her on the carpet on it. I know exactly how much she loves what I do to her.

"I'm grateful for your overprotective quality, though," Joslyn says, her smile turning soft with a tint of sadness to it.

"I would think it would make you happy, kitten," I say, taking her hand in mine. "You know I will never let anything bad happen to you.

Her gaze roams my face, her smile curving a little deeper. "I know that."

"Never," I reiterate, leaning in closer to her.

"Never ever?" she asks softly, head tilted in wonder.

It's a question asking for a commitment. While we've only been reconnected for a brief time, the void of those twelve years seems to have vanished for me.

Has it for her?

I reply to her question, making a promise I have no qualms in giving. "Never ever."

Her hand jerks reflexively in mine, but I just tighten my grip. She regards me with wide, questioning eyes. I can see deep within… she's afraid to believe in what I just proclaimed.

"Joslyn." My voice is gruff, laced with emotion and a distinct understanding I don't know how to put this all into words. "I hate you're going through this but fuck… part of me is glad. It's what led you back to me. And we've realized that big mistakes were made long ago, but I think we've both realized we never moved on after we broke up. That has to mean something."

"No," she agrees with a smile. "I never moved on."

"I sure as fuck didn't," I mutter before bending my neck so I can brush my mouth across hers. When I pull back, I make sure her eyes are on me for what I'm about to say next. "You're it for me, Jos. It was always only ever you. And here you are again—*mine*—and I'd be a fucking fool to let you go."

"Oh, Kynan," she murmurs as tears fill her eyes. "I don't want you to let go. I don't want to let go. It's so funny… I've never been more scared or vulnerable in my life, and yet—especially these last few days—I've never been happier. I've fallen in love with you all over again."

"Christ," I mutter, the enormity of those words

washing over me. Jerking her into my arms, I settle her in my lap. "I love you, too, kitten."

I remember back to the first time I'd heard words of love from her beautiful lips. It was in the lobby of the Jameson offices in Vegas. Joslyn had chosen to pass on a movie deal that would require her to move to Los Angeles. She didn't decline because of me, but because it didn't feel right to her. Her passion was singing, not acting, and it was the first time she'd ever defied her mother.

She came straight to Jameson, we declared our love for each other, and I promptly moved her into my apartment. Three days later, Joslyn broke it off with me after her mother showed her the fake investigative report.

Just a few days after that, she was living in Los Angeles and doing the movie she didn't want to do.

"How are we going to make this work?" Joslyn asked. "I mean... apart from the lunatic who is after me, we live on opposite sides of the continent."

"I expect we'll be traveling a lot, kitten," I reply with a smile. "Let's dispatch this fucker first, then we'll get busy figuring things out."

"Okay," she says with what I'd term to be a dopey grin. I don't see a single line of stress caused by this fucker who has been terrorizing her. It's beyond exhilarating I can cause that level of happiness within her, despite everything that's going on.

CHAPTER 24

Joslyn

"**Y**OUR CHARIOT AWAITS, milady," Cruce says in the worst British accent I've ever heard. He smiles rakishly as he opens the passenger door.

I glance at my front door, see Kynan watching us as he leans against the doorjamb, arms folded over his chest. He shakes his head and smiles before disappearing inside. Some guy is coming to interview with him this morning for a position at Jameson, so he's not joining us.

"Thank you, kind sir," I tease with a mock curtsy before sliding into the seat. Cruce is just one of those guys who is easy to like and joke with.

He shuts the door and I fish my phone out of my purse, wanting to send a quick text to my mom to let her know we're on the way. It's a short five-minute drive from my house to the Four Seasons.

I swipe up on my screen, let the facial recognition do its thing, then move to my texts. *On our way. Be there in five.*

A reply chimes almost immediately, too soon for my mom to have responded. It's from an unknown number and I almost don't read it, but the first line not only catches my attention, but it also holds me hostage with mind-numbing fear.

I have your manager, and I will kill her if…

Tapping on the message, I bring the full message up.

I have your manager, and I will kill her if you don't do exactly as I say. When you get to the Four Seasons, head through to the north end of the lobby. There's an alcove with phones near a service entrance door. Go out that door. Turn right. Walk through the employee parking lot. I'll be waiting for you.

A photo of Lynn is the next message to pop up.

Oh my God.

She's tied to a chair in a semi-dark room with duct tape over her mouth. Her hands are bound behind her back, and she looks terrified.

I make a small sound of distress deep in my throat.

"You okay?" Cruce asks affably.

"Um… yeah," I reply dismissively as another text comes in below the picture.

Time is of the essence. I am following you right now. If you don't come to the spot I've described immediately, I will leave and kill Lynn.

Jesus, no. No, no, no.

I glance over at Cruce, noting his right hand propped casually on the wheel. Do I tell him what's going on? There's no way in hell he'll let me meet this lunatic. He'll hold me back, insist on calling Kynan in, and Lynn will die.

I don't dare turn around to search for the car my stalker is in. I don't doubt him for a second.

I read through the messages again. As I study Lynn's face, I know I cannot let her die.

Shakily, I type a quick message back to him. *Okay.*

Good girl, he responds.

The Four Seasons is up ahead. I quickly type one more text, but I don't send it.

My heart is galloping out of control as we pull up to the front entrance. I can see my mom coming through the lobby to the front doors. Making a split-second decision, I hop out of the car, slinging my purse over my shoulder. "I have to use the bathroom, Cruce. I'll be right back."

"Wait a minute," he calls through the open door. "Let me just park and I'll go in with you."

I give him what I hope is a charming, carefree smile. "What... you think my stalker is waiting in the lobby of the Four Seasons on the off chance I'll be strolling in? I'll be fine. Be back in like two minutes."

"Joslyn... damn it. Just wait a second and let me park—"

After I shut the door, cutting him off, I hold up two fingers, mouthing the words, "Two minutes." I can't hear him, but I can see him cursing.

But I don't have time to spare him another glance. I hop the curb, trot to the lobby doors, then make my way inside just as my mom arrives.

"Joslyn..." Beaming, she opens her arms wide. We just had dinner last night, her and Darren having flown in on a late-afternoon flight, but no one would know it by her greeting.

Giving her a hard, quick hug, I whisper fiercely in her ear. "I love you."

Laughing, she squeezes me. "I love you, too, honey."

After I release her, I give her a tiny push to the door. Cruce is out of the car, trying valiantly to hand the keys off to a valet attendant who is trying to get in another car, and I need to hurry.

Pivoting to my mom, I urge her along. "Go out there and tell Cruce not to bother parking the car. I'll be right back out, okay?"

"Okay, sweetie," she chirps, then disappears in a cloud of Chanel perfume.

Half-walking, half-jogging, I make my way across the expanse of red tiles in the lobby. Straight to the alcove he described.

I don't break stride, continuing right to the service door he'd said would be there. Gripping my phone hard in one hand, I push through and blink at the bright sunlight. I'm disoriented a moment, forgetting what he told me to do.

Then it hits me.

Right.

He said turn right.

I do, blindly moving past a stucco half wall housing several HVAC units that are blowing loudly. The thundering of my heart within my own ears almost drowns it out, though.

There's a small parking lot with about twenty or so cars in two rows. I edge slowly down the first row, not sure what I'm even searching for.

But then… a black economy car pulls into the row ahead of me, slowly heading my way. I step to the left, willingly putting myself on the passenger side as it approaches.

Knowing I'm getting in that damn car with him.

It comes to a stop, and the window rolls down. Bending, I get my first real look at my tormentor.

I'm stunned by how normal he looks. Plain face, neither ugly nor handsome. Normal—with sandy-blond hair cut short and combed neat, mud-brown eyes, and thin lips. I had expected him to look like a monster. Maybe scarred. Deformed, perhaps. He was wearing a mask when he attacked me, and I always felt it had to do with more than just thwarting identification.

"Hello, Jos," he says, and the hair on the nape of my neck rises. I recognize his voice. "Get in the car."

Staring in the direction I just walked from, I half expect—and really want—to see Cruce bursting out the service door.

"You've got five seconds, Joslyn," my stalker says, and my head snaps his way. "Otherwise, I'm leaving, and Lynn will soon be a dead woman. I'll drive off, go to where I have her, and slit her throat. Before she dies, I'll make sure she knows you could have saved her. And when it's all said and done, I'm coming after you again. And that sure was long winded on my part, so your five seconds are up. Get in the car. Now."

I jump, reaching for the door handle.

"Get rid of the purse and phone," he says.

I glance at my phone—at my message typed and ready to go. A sharp pain hits me in the center of my chest for everything that's probably becoming lost to me in this very moment. My thumb taps the send icon, and the message whooshes away.

My phone falls from my hands. I shrug, making my purse land beside it. After I open the door and slide into the passenger seat, I feel physically sick to my stomach to be sitting so close to him.

I force myself to face him. "You swear you'll let Lynn go?"

"Scout's honor," he says with a leering grin.

"You have no honor," I snap.

The smile slides from his face, and he bares his teeth. "When I finish with you, you won't be so sassy."

His eyes roam over my face, and I pray he doesn't focus in on my earrings. They're my only link to Kynan.

He doesn't pay them any mind. Instead, he says, "Put on your seatbelt."

I do as he says, woodenly pulling it across my chest and clicking it into place.

"I'm sorry for this," he says, and I'm surprised by the genuine remorse in his tone.

"Sorry about what?" I grit out, seething with anger he'd dare to apologize for his atrocities.

"About this," he says, and I feel a sharp pinch in my upper arm. A syringe is plunged in to the hilt. When he pulls it out, my head swims. I'm immediately dizzy, and it's hard to focus on his face. "Sorry I have to drug you. I like it when you fight, but I need you docile for now."

"Fuck you," I try to snarl, but the words are thick and slurred. He's amused. I can tell by his laugh. It's the last thing I hear before darkness takes me.

CHAPTER 25

Kynan

WHEN THE DOORBELL rings, I leave my spot at the kitchen island, which has become my makeshift office since I've been at Joslyn's house. She offered me her office, but I didn't want to disrupt her normal flow of work throughout the day. She spends a lot of time in there, jotting down notes for new song lyrics and playing tunes she made up in her head on a keyboard set up in the corner, which she translates into written music.

I make my way to the front door, disable the alarm, and open it to find Saint Bellinger standing there.

I don't know much about the man. He's as mysterious as the night, but he comes with good references. The main one is from my former business partner, Jerico Jameson, whom I bought my company from. Jerico served with Saint briefly in the Marine Corps. He's apparently a master of breaking into places and moving about unseen. Due to the fact he's had military training, it makes him a prime recruitment opportunity for me.

Saint is immediately distinguished by the fact he's

wearing a custom-tailored suit that probably costs more than what most people make in a month. His dark hair is perfectly styled. Despite his large build, he stands there with grace. Smiling, I stick my hand out. "Kynan McGrath."

His return grip is sure and strong. "Saint Bellinger."

I move out of the threshold, beckoning him into Joslyn's house. Once he's in, I close the door, resetting the alarm.

He notices this, nodding at the security panel. "Not often I see a well-accomplished male feel the need to arm the security system while he's home in broad daylight."

Chuckling, I pivot away from him, walking into the kitchen. "It's become force of habit. I'm constantly on my girlfriend's case to make sure it stays armed at all times."

The minute the word "girlfriend" rolls off my tongue, a warm feeling pulses through me. I realize how immediately accepting I am of the concept Joslyn is truly mine again.

What other titles will I have for her? Fiancée? Wife? Best friend? Lover? Co-parent?

None of that freaks me out. Instead, it all feels very, very right.

"Would you like a cup of coffee?" I ask as Saint follows me into the kitchen.

"Sure. Black."

As I set about to make him a cup of java, I fill him in on Joslyn and her stalker. When I finish, I say, "That's why I'm here in California. But I'll be headed back to Pittsburgh as soon as this case is wrapped up."

"I'm interested to hear more about your company," Saint remarks as he takes a seat at the kitchen island. "Jerico tells me you're going in a new direction from what he originally envisioned."

I chuckle, leaning my forearms on the countertop opposite of where he sits. "No offense to Jerico. He's my best friend. But let's just say I was getting a little tired of installing security systems and providing bodyguard services to celebrities with big egos and low self-esteem."

Saint takes a sip of his coffee. After he sets the mug down, he asks point blank. "How exciting is the work you anticipate doing going to be?"

I shrug. "Anything from rescuing a kidnap victim from a South American jungle to stealing shit from America's known enemies. It's totally off-the-books stuff our government doesn't want to be associated with but will gladly pay to have done."

Saint nods in understanding at the same time my phone buzzes on the counter where I left it next to my laptop. I glance down, seeing a notification Joslyn has sent me a text.

Granted, while this interview is pretty informal, I am still in the middle of a business dealing and would ordinarily ignore such a thing.

But it's Joslyn.

And knowing her, she is probably sending me something silly and designed only to make me smile.

I should ignore it.

But it's Joslyn.

"Excuse me," I say to Saint as I reach out to take my phone. After I tap on the text, I start to read, my body locking tight. In an instant, I feel like my entire life has just been shattered.

I'm so sorry, Kynan. He has Lynn. He's going to kill her if I don't go with him. I had to make a quick decision. No matter what happens, I love you so very much. Please forgive me for what I'm getting ready to do.

A wave of nausea hits me as I realize the kiss I gave Joslyn just before she walked out the door with Cruce may have been the last time I ever touch her. This text may be the last words she ever says to me.

He could be killing her right this very moment.

My phone rings in my hand. I'm so startled I almost drop it. Cruce's name comes up on the screen, and I answer it by barking, "What the fuck is going on? I just got a text from Joslyn that sounds like she willingly went with the bastard."

Saint stands up from the stool opposite me, his body tight and hyper alert as he watches me with concern.

"She ditched me at the Four Seasons," Cruce grits out with anger and frustration. "Hopped out of the fucking car and said she had to use the bathroom. Ran off as I was trying to get out of the car. I swear to God, Kynan, I couldn't have been more than ten seconds behind her, but she wasn't in the bathrooms. She just disappeared."

"I don't fucking understand," I say as I snag the keys to the car I rented when I first arrived in Santa Barbara. Saint follows along behind me as I head to the door, but I pay him no mind. "I'm on my way to you now."

"I've already called the police. They should be arriving any moment. I'm in the employee parking lot off the service door from the lobby. I found her purse and phone. Saw a car pulling away pretty fast, and I managed to get a partial license plate on it, but I couldn't see if she was in there or not."

"Jesus fucking Christ," I mutter. I'm so angry with Joslyn right now for doing this... and at Cruce for letting her. My head is fogged up, and my ability to form rational thought is impaired.

And then it hits me, just as I reach the front door.

I disconnect from Cruce without another word, pulling up the tracking app I installed. It's connected to the devices in her purse, phone, and in the earrings I gave her. Christ, was she wearing the earrings today? I can't remember. Her hair was loose and covered her ears, but I'd told her to always wear them. Surely, she had, right?

"What is that?" Saint answers as he steps in to look

closer at my app.

"A tracking device."

"He's got your woman?" he asks.

"She apparently got in his car willingly because he said he'd taken her manager," I grit out, furious still at Joslyn but also incredibly terrified at the same time.

"Says a lot about your woman," Saint remarks, and I glare at him. He just shrugs. "She must have a lot of love and loyalty to have done that."

Yeah... She sure as fuck does, but I'm furious at her for being that way.

I tap on the icon that will connect to the signal in Joslyn's earrings. The purse and phone are out of play, but with my breath caught in my throat, I wait for a red flashing circle to come up on the Google maps the app integrates. I get nothing in return.

"Shit," I mutter.

"What's the signal distance?" Saint asks.

"Ten miles." That was the problem when we had the earrings created on such short notice—we were only able to use readily available technology. The size of chip we put in the earrings has only so much strength in its signal.

The lack of a signal tells me something particularly important, though.

Which direction he is headed.

If he was headed south toward Joslyn's house from

the Four Seasons, I would have picked up the signal. It's proof he's headed either north or west, which at least gives me a starting point.

I spare Saint a glance to say, "Sorry, buddy. Interview's over. We'll have to pick this back up some other time."

"I'd like to help," Saint says. "I can't learn a damsel is in distress and just walk away."

I nod gratefully, quickly disarming the security panel so we can exit the house. "I'll shoot you the link so you can download this app. Follow me in your car to the Four Seasons. Once there, you, Cruce and I will branch out to search for her."

In seconds, I'm in my car headed to the Four Seasons. I place a call to Bebe.

I come to appreciate her efficiency even more when she answers my call by giving me an immediate update. "I've already talked to Cruce. Rachel and I have the map up. Once her signal comes online, I'll sync it to the app so everyone can have access to it. In the meantime, I'm running the partial license plate Cruce was able to get. I had to hack the California's Department of Motor Vehicles so if I get caught, you have to bail me out."

"I've got your back, Bebe. Thank you for jumping on this so fast."

I disconnect the call, driving like a bat out of hell... knowing the clock is ticking way too fast.

CHAPTER 26

Joslyn

I COME GROGGILY awake for what feels like the third or fourth time, struggling to keep my eyes open. Wherever I am, it is almost pitch black around me. I can tell I'm in a chair with my hands tied behind the back. Moving my legs is impossible. It feels like my ankles are tied to each of the front legs of the chair with rope.

I'm also really cold, and I think my clothes have been removed.

In front of me is a thin, bright line running horizontally where I believe the floor meets the doorway. I'm feeling incredibly tired, my eyes wanting to drift shut again. The darkness presses heavily upon me, making me want to give back to sleep.

But then I hear something. Or perhaps I just feel a presence.

Horrible wrenching sounds—like metal is being ripped apart—screech through my ears, then white light floods the darkness.

It's so bright that pain shoots through my head, and

I have to snap my eyes shut against it. I can feel a thin veil of warmth hit my body, so it must be sunlight. When I manage to flutter my eyelids open, a person is silhouetted in the doorway.

Without a doubt, it's *him*.

He stands there facing me. Even though I can't see the details of his face, I can't bear to look at him. My head drops and I take in my body, noticing I am indeed naked except for my bra and panties. My legs are spread slightly due to the fact they are tied to the front chair legs.

No clue what he has done to me.

I try for an internal evaluation to see if I'm feeling pain anywhere.

I'm not, except for a dull headache. I don't feel anything throughout my body as I try to flex muscles, but it doesn't mean he didn't rape me. Still, I have to believe if he had, he would have just left me naked. At least that's my hope, but I can't dwell on that now. I have more important things to worry about—like staying alive.

My stalker steps forward, then reaches out and flips a switch. An overhead light comes on directly above me, illuminating a bare bulb hanging from a socket. The man pulls the door shut behind himself, the hinges sounding like groaning steel. All of a sudden, I realize I'm in a metal shipping container about the size of a standard bedroom.

"Where am I?" I ask, my tongue thick and heavy in my mouth. It's an effort to form words.

The man is standing just beyond the scope of light. I have to admit, he's more terrifying standing in the shadows than if he were right in my face. He gives a dark chuckle. "Why, you're at my home."

"You live in a steel box?" I snap.

He laughs again, totally amused by my defiance. "Of course not, my beautiful girl. I live in a house. But you are on land that encompasses my home, so that might be the better way to say it."

"What did you do to me?" I ask, concerned at how much of an effort it is to talk. My words are heavy and slurred, and I struggle to make sure they sound coherent.

My kidnapper takes a step forward, then another. I shrink back as far as I can. When he comes into the scope of light, I realize he is more terrifying close up than when he was in the shadows. It all comes back to me—the normalcy of this man. How common he appears. He could be anybody. The fact he does not resemble a monster makes him all the more frightening.

He squats before me, placing his hands on my thighs just above my kneecaps. Bile rises in my throat from his touch. "I gave you Midazolam. It's a short-acting sedative that should wear off soon."

"Why? I got in the car as you asked. Why did you have to drug me?"

Snorting, the bastard shakes his head. "I really couldn't have you struggling against me. You put up a hell of a fight the last time we met, so it's with my deepest apologies I had to do that."

A sharp, hysterical laugh bubbles up. "Apologize? You've tried to kill me once already. You've kidnapped me. And now you're apologizing?"

His expression goes horrified at my accusation. Shaking his head, he says, "No, no, no. I didn't try to kill you that first time, sweet girl. I just wanted you unconscious so I could... do things to you. I didn't want to hit you on the head—maybe risk brain damage. And let me remind you that you willingly got in my car. I didn't kidnap you."

That's just semantics, but then it hits me what he said. I *did* get in the car with him willingly, but that was because he has Lynn.

Terror jolts through my body. I jerk hard against my bindings, scanning wildly around the interior of the shipping container. I scream, "Lynn. Lynn, are you here?"

The man squeezes my legs reassuringly before he stands. "Calm down, Joslyn. She's not here."

I snap my head around, glaring with disbelief. "Where is she? What have you done to her? You promised you would let her go."

"I didn't need to let her go," he drawls with a mischievous twinkle in his eye. "Because I never had her in the first place."

My brain turns fuzzy again, trying to understand the meaning behind his words. "What? I don't understand."

The asshole bends and puts his face near mine. The smell of stale coffee hits me hard. His grin is leering. "Of course you don't understand. Because you're stupid, Joslyn. I never had Lynn. Did you ever stop to think that maybe I sent you a fake photo? That I had doctored it up? Did you not once consider that if I was good enough to hack into city cameras so you and your merry band of fake detectives couldn't find me, that I could doctor up a single fucking photo? You're so goddamn gullible, Joslyn, and you made this so easy. In fact, if I didn't know any better, I'd say you wanted me to take you."

My entire body sags into the chair as I realize I probably just destroyed my life, and probably Kynan's as well, because I didn't trust in him. I didn't trust in the process of him protecting me. I fell for this asshole's lie so damn easily and it also occurs to me that I will probably deserve everything I'm in for.

Head drooping, I stare at my pale thighs under the glaring light. My voice is tired and raspy. "Why me?"

The man straightens, then starts a slow walk around my chair. "Now that *is* a good question. Why you?"

He moves from my line of vision. When he comes up behind me, I brace for him to do something as sinister as slitting my throat or as creepy as just touching me. Instead, all I hear is his voice coming from the darkness.

"I attended a concert of yours a few years ago. Sprang for front-row seats. You were singing right to me, Joslyn. You stared me right in the eyes, and you sang only for me. And I felt the connection between us."

I start shaking my head. "I don't remember you at all. I perform. I act. It's what I do. There's no connection."

The man slides around to my front. His eyes are hard and cold. "Careful, Joslyn. Else I won't have any use for you if you stop being nice."

His threat is clear, and a smarter woman might become subdued. But I've about reached my limit of his torment, which is exactly what he's doing to me. He is terrorizing me with his singsong tone and teasing words.

Straightening in my chair, I lean my head and torso as far forward as I can, lifting my chin in defiance. "You are sick. Demented. What type of man has to tie up a woman to get what he wants? I'll tell you... it's a psychopathic creep who probably has a little dick and—"

His hand cocks back quickly and he lets it fly, catching me with his palm across my left cheek. The blow is so forceful my head snaps to the right, the chair actually leaning onto two legs before it corrects itself. There's an immediate ringing in my ears, and my vision starts to dim.

And then, he strikes me again. In the same exact way, an open palm to my left cheek.

This blow is harder. My teeth slice into my cheek, causing blood to flood my mouth. I gag against the taste, tilting to the side to spit it out. When I look back up, my insides turn to ice. He has a switchblade open, and he's holding it up for me to see.

"If you want me to get nasty with you, Joslyn, I will. Or you can be a good, quiet little bitch. If you are, I won't hurt you too much."

I am effectively put my place.

"Okay, okay, okay." I make my voice as meek and subservient as I can muster. It's not too hard, since I am genuinely terrified now. "I'm sorry. I'm just scared and disoriented, and I don't feel good. I'm sorry."

He stares, his cold beady eyes calculating the weight of my words. Finally, and ever so slowly, he closes the knife and puts it away. A huge rush of air forcefully exhales from my lungs when it disappears.

I muster up the courage, asking the one question I'm terrified to know the answer to. "What are you going to do to me?"

He bends again, putting his face in front of mine. Blood continues to fill my mouth. I can't lean over and spit it out without most likely offending him. Instead, I swallow the vileness, hoping to God I don't wretch it back up.

He reaches a hand out, then runs a finger tenderly over my left cheekbone, which is burning like unholy fire from where he hit me. He murmurs, "I'm going to make you my pet. I'll keep you for as long as you amuse and please me. And when I'm sick of you, I'll get rid of you. My advice is to be good and make me happy. If you can manage that, maybe I'll keep you for a while."

Sickening awareness overtakes me. "You've done this before, haven't you? You told me that I would be your favorite."

The man grins before standing. He punches both of his hands into his front pockets. "Well, you *have* made it interesting. I've definitely enjoyed the challenge. And you've been a bad girl by making time with another man. I don't forgive you for that, you know. I'm going to hurt you because of it. But eventually, you'll come to love me, Joslyn."

Self-preservation be damned. "You're delusional. You might as well kill me now because I will never submit to you. I'll never give you what you want without a fight every step of the way."

"Oh, contraire," he teases. "You'll beg me eventual-ly."

"Never," I hiss.

This amuses him, which pisses me off because I seem to do that a lot. Turning his back on me, he laughs dismissively as he retreats to the door. "That's the drugs talking. Giving you false courage. I'm going to wait for it to get out of your system before we begin. In the meantime, I'm just going to leave you here in the dark and let you think about things."

He reaches out for the light switch.

"Wait," I cry.

He turns to regard me.

I plead with him. "Don't turn the lights out."

I'm ashamed I'm already begging him for something.

It's made even worse by the fact he doesn't give me what I asked for. Instead, he flips the switch. He opens the door, giving me one last burst of light, then he leaves and closes it behind him.

I can't hold back the tears as I'm plunged into darkness.

CHAPTER 27

Kynan

T HE FOUR SEASONS is an absolute zoo when I get there. There are several police cars in front of the hotel and on the side of the employee parking lot where I pull my car around to meet Cruce. They already have yellow tape marking off the area where she was abducted. Yellow plastic cones have been placed on the ground beside her purse and cell phone. A technician is taking photos.

Cruce meets me at my car door as I exit. I make a quick introduction between him and Saint when he joins us.

"I am so fucking sorry," Cruce says, and I can't stand the remorse in his voice. It's almost as if he doesn't have any hope we will find her, but I'm also wise enough to know he is speaking from an emotional place just as I am.

"Did you get anything from her phone before the police got here?" I ask.

Nodding, Cruce pulls his own phone out. "Yeah.

The text she sent you was still visible on her screen, and I took some pictures."

He pulls up the images, and I read the exchange Joslyn had with her stalker. My gut burns so badly I'm afraid I might double over and vomit because it was so fucking easy for him to get her. I'd never in a million years imagined he would try to trick Joslyn into voluntarily going with him.

And that's squarely on my fucking shoulders, not Cruce's.

I have to admit—he hit her right in her tender spot. Kidnapping Lynn, Harry, or her mother would have guaranteed she'd get in that car. I'm angrier with myself than I could ever be with Cruce over this happening. I should have prepared her better.

"Kynan." Madeline's voice comes from behind me, and I spin around to see her bolting straight at me with Darren right behind her. Her face is red, her eyes are wet, and she looks like she is in exquisite pain. This is the face of a woman who believes her daughter could be dead.

She throws herself in my arms. I immediately and protectively—since she is Joslyn's mother—envelop her in a hug.

Immediately pulling away, she starts babbling. "You have got to find her. It all happened so fast. She just went inside to use the bathroom, and I didn't think anything of it. Cruce did, though. We followed her in, but she was just gone. She knew what she was doing. If I'd known, I would've stopped her."

Shaking my head, I give Madeline an empathetic smile. "You wouldn't have been able to stop her. Neither could Cruce. The stalker sent her a text before she got to the hotel, and she had planned it all out. She was determined to escape and go with him. It's nobody's fault."

Except mine. I'm going to take all the blame for this one since I did not impress upon Joslyn how she should trust me and only me. It makes me wonder if the declarations we made to each other yesterday about wanting to be together are rooted in any type of reality. Shouldn't she have trusted me without me having to tell her to do so?

On the flip side, she was hit with a major decision and she was given no time to reason it out. I can understand that as well. Maybe I would have done the same thing in her shoes.

I can't worry about that now. There is still plenty of opportunity to get her back, and that's what I'm going to do.

I move my hands to her shoulders. "Time is of the essence, Madeline. I'm going after her right now."

She nods, sniffles, and lets Darren pull her into his embrace.

I turn to Cruce and Saint. "We have no time to waste. We've got to move out now to catch up to the signal."

"Just tell us what to do," Saint says.

"We need to hit the road and move in different directions," Cruce says, studying the tracking app on his phone. "With only a ten-mile radius on that signal, we have got to go *now*."

"Agreed," I say, my eyes going back and forth between the men. "Bebe has sent each of us updated maps with individualized routes to take. When one of us connects to Joslyn's signal, Bebe will sync the location to everyone's maps. We're going to discount heading south since the signal never appeared on my phone as I traveled here from Joslyn's house."

"That could be because he made her ditch the earrings," Cruce points out.

"I know that." My words are gruff. "But there's only three of us and a lot of miles. We have to make an educated deduction and just work north right now."

"Let's do it," Cruce says.

We break apart to head to our vehicles. A man I recognize as Detective Kitchner heads toward me from an unmarked patrol car. He holds a hand up and waves, indicating he wants to talk.

I don't have time for it. Taking three steps toward him, I say, "I don't have time to talk to you. Joslyn has a tracking device on her body. I will have my people send you the link once we get it. If you can send patrol cars out, that would be great."

"I have just a few questions," Kitchner says.

Shaking my head, I hold up a palm to stop him. "Can't. I'm leaving now. If you want to help, get your men out there to search for her."

He opens his mouth as if he wants to say something extremely important, but I turn my back on him and he doesn't utter another word. As soon as I get in my car, I pull up the map Bebe sent me and take off.

Bebe has me going up Highway 154, otherwise known as the San Marcos Pass Road, which ascends the northern portion of the Santa Ynez Mountains. It's the least populated portion of the area. If this psychopath wants privacy, this is probably my best bet.

When my phone rings, I'm startled for a moment. I see it's Jerico calling, but I doubt he's calling to offer sage advice or a scathingly brilliant idea on how to capture this bastard.

He's calling to offer moral support.

I connect the call. "Are you calling to tell me everything is going to be all right?"

"I would if I could, buddy," he says. Taking a moment, he clears his throat. "I just want to let you know I'm jumping on a plane. I'll be there soon."

"Nothing you can do, mate. If we find her, it's going

to have to be done quickly, before you can make it in to help."

"I'm not coming for her," he says softly. "I'm coming for you. I sure as shit don't know what's going to happen, but I'm coming for you."

I'm beyond touched. If I'm possibly facing the worst outcome, which I dare not even consider at this point, there's no one I would want by my side other than Jerico. "I could try to talk you out of this, but I know it will be useless and I don't have time to waste. So safe travels. I'll see you when you get here."

◆

MIRACULOUSLY, IT'S LESS than ten minutes later when my phone issues a chime, which is followed by a gloriously beautiful blinking dot on the Google map about nine miles from me.

Joslyn.

My phone immediately rings. When I connect it, Bebe speaks with her trademark efficiency. Of course she's on top of the fact we have found Joslyn.

"Kynan... I've got you on a conference call with both Cruce and Saint. Everybody's phones are now synced up to her signal. Even though they are slightly out of range, they'll be able to see it through your phone's connection."

"Saint and I are adjusting course to head for the

signal," Cruce says.

"Sounds good," I reply. "Bebe... get up with Detective Kitchner and let him know."

"On it," she replies and promptly disconnects.

I'm left on the phone with Saint and Cruce.

"I'm assuming it would be a waste of breath to tell you to wait for us when you get there," Cruce says.

"Yeah, that would be pretty stupid, mate," I answer, and I can't help but smile. I'm so relieved to have her signal that I'm feeling practically jubilant at this point.

"I'm going to find her," I tell them. "And when I do, I'm going after *him*. If you happen to make it there in time, I'm ordering you both to stand down. Don't try to stop me."

There's a moment of silence before Cruce says, "Wouldn't think of it."

"Saint?" I ask.

"You're not my boss," he says. "Not yet, anyway. But I'll stand down."

That's good enough for me.

I'm coming, Joslyn.

Just hang tight.

CHAPTER 28

Joslyn

*M*Y *MOUNTAIN HOME is beautiful. It's nothing like I had ever envisioned having. When I thought about marriage and kids, I'd expected to live in a cute Victorian cottage with a white picket fence. Instead, I live in the rolling foothills under the shadow of the beautiful mountain city of Pittsburgh. In addition to the dog I'd always wanted, I've got two cats and a goldfish.*

Two beautiful children as well. A boy and a girl, six and eight, and I stare at them through my office window as they run around outside with our golden retriever, Lucy.

My heart is out there—wrapped up in those kids. Miniature replicas of my husband and me.

The crunch of gravel catches my attention, and my gaze sweeps to a long driveway that leads out to a rural road. It's Kynan's Jeep, and my heart sings out to the man approaching.

The one who gave me my true happy ending.

I push up from my desk, taking a moment to save the new song lyrics I was working on, and make my way through the house. It's a mountain cabin built of pine and pitch, and I love it so much. It's the first place I've lived in that has seemed like a true home.

Just as I make my way onto the front porch, Kynan steps out of his Jeep. Before he can shut the door, the kids throw themselves at him.

Strange. I know they're my children, but I can't recall their names. I just know I love them in a way I could never love my husband.

Not more. Not less.

Simply in a different way.

Kynan's head rises, his eyes locking with mine across the front yard. Smiling, I hurry off the porch where he reaches to pull me into the family embrace.

He kisses my cheek and says, "I missed you today."

"I missed you, too." Grinning, I give him a slight tickle on his ribs. "I have to change the air filter in the upstairs hallway, but it's too high up."

Kynan frowns and shakes his head. "You don't need my help to do that."

I frown right back. "Yes, I do. It's too high for me to reach, and you need to do it."

"Joslyn," he chides. "I can't always be here to help you do things. You're just going to have to figure it out on your own."

The words punch through me. For a moment, I think he's being inconsiderate of my feelings.

And then I realize... I can do it on my own.

I snap wide awake, blinking into the darkness. The last of the sedative has worn away, and my mind is finally clear. Without any struggle to remember, I know I am tied to a chair in a shipping container and I'm being held at the whim of a madman.

I also know my dream just gave me the answer to what should have been my first cognizant question upon waking up. "What the hell do I do now?"

I have to figure out how to get out of here.

The first and obviously the most pressing issue is the fact I'm tied to a chair. When the man had come into the container and turned on the light, I hadn't bothered to try to see the bonds around my ankles. It feels like rope, and there's no sense in struggling to figure it out now since it's too dark to see anything. But my ankles can wait. I need to free my hands, so I twist my wrists and feel about with my fingertips. I'm able to touch what feels like silken rope, wrapped many times around me in several knots. There's no way I can maneuver my hands so my fingers can work at the knots. It's just too tight.

My mind races, trying to remember if I ever learned anything from watching MacGyver about how to help me out of this situation. Without a paper clip, it seems hopeless.

I'm just going to have to use brute strength and determination to get out of my restraints.

Twisting, turning, and pulling, I use the muscles in

my arms to try to wrench my wrists apart for some distance to stretch my bindings. The ropes are incredibly tight, but unless it's my imagination, I feel like there might be some give. I envision becoming free, opening the crate, and running, running, running. My end goal is to reach somewhere safe where I can call Kynan and the police. At which point, they can arrest this bastard and free me from this nightmare.

It's good motivation.

I work harder, sawing my hands back and forth as much as I can under the restraints. Before long, my skin is burning. The burn turns to true pain as I pull, struggle, and groan and grunt, tears pricking my eyes.

"Come on, you motherfucking bastard," I scream. The words are released into the darkness, but they give me added strength. I start to really move my wrists under the bonds. Thankfully, the pain eventually gives way to a bit of numbness, which lets me keep working hard at my task.

Then I feel wetness.

What is that? Water?

No. Blood.

I'm bleeding.

Self-preservation kicks in. I consider stopping. Can I bleed to death?

Of course not, Joslyn. That's ridiculous. Keep working.

My chest heaves with the effort. Tears flow freely

down my face, a mixture of pain and frustration. I viciously twist and turn my wrists, this way and that, until there is a distinct popping sound. For a moment, I think I dislocated something. When there is no rush of pain to accompany it, I realize the ropes have loosened significantly. I think one of the loops may have slipped over a knot creating some space.

The immediate appearance of slack in my restraints rejuvenates me, and I work even more furiously. I'm breathing so hard I'm afraid I'm going to hyperventilate, so I try to center myself. "Come on you bastard. Loosen up."

Suddenly, one wrist comes completely free. When I pull my arm up, a sharp stab of pain hits me in that shoulder, rushing up the side of my neck. I breathe through it, telling myself it's nothing more than the strange position my arms have been locked in for God knows how long.

Taking several deep breaths, I push past the hurt, moving my other wrist out of the loosened ropes. Much more slowly, I pull my arm forward, wincing through the ache in that shoulder. Rolling my head and shoulders to loosen them, I take a few more breaths.

"Okay, Joslyn. You can do this."

Bending forward and leaning to the right, I work on my right ankle restraints. My fingers are slippery from the blood that coats them, and I immediately become frustrated with how tight the knots are. I break several nails trying to loosen them, and a string of curses fly out of my mouth.

But I don't give up. Kynan would not want me to give up.

Time has no concept. It could've taken me thirty seconds or thirty minutes, but I eventually manage to pull the last rope off my ankles. I immediately lurch up from the chair, then regret it as a wave of dizziness hits me. My stomach rolls, and I sink back onto the wooden seat. I focus on the bright beam of horizontal light that represents the door out of my prison.

Taking a deep breath, I rise slowly once more. I take a tentative step, then another, with my arms stretched in front of me until I reach the door. Remembering the switch is no more than a foot off from the hinge, I let my fingers feel around the cold metal wall until I find it. When the bulb illuminates, I take a second to issue a prayer of thanks. Then I pivot and scan the storage container, taking in everything I could not see the first time the man was here.

The hair on the nape of my neck rises at what I see behind the chair I was tied to.

A hospital bed pushed flush against the back wall, which is accompanied by stirrups that stand out lewdly from the bottom corners. Next to it is a surgical tray on a rolling cart. Upon the tray is a slew of metal implements—scalpels, ice picks, and pliers are only the beginning. On the wall are two wooden shelves containing a variety of sex toys, whips, and chains.

A full-body shudder overtakes me as the magnitude of what this man intends to do to me hits. It's a torture I had not ever dared to imagine. A wave of sheer and utter panic to escape slices through me. I turn and bolt for the door, relieved to see the lock is a two-sided bar that just lifts up. It's hinged through a hole in the door, meaning when I lift it from this side, it will mimic a bar on the outside. I have no clue if it's locked, but I reach out to give it a go.

Then I freeze. I have no clue what's on the other side.

It could be my attacker with that amused fucking smile on his face, just waiting for me to walk right through and into his arms.

Spinning around, I take in the interior once more. I specifically search for my clothing, but I don't see any of it. What I do see, though, are several weapons I can use to defend myself. I rush over to the surgical tray, immediately grabbing one of the ice picks. For some reason, I decide that's not good enough and return it, picking up a scalpel instead. I have no experience with which to go on, but something tells me I'll have an easier time slicing rather than stabbing.

Just as I'm about to turn for the door, something on

one of the shelves catches my eye. A Taser. I recognize it because I have one in my house. I lunge for it, grabbing the base and holding it up to the light so I can examine it.

Yes, it will work nicely.

I carefully push the scalpel into the front of my bra, right at the center of my chest. It's the tightest spot that will hopefully hold the weapon in place in case I need it later. Gripping the Taser in my dominant hand, I make for the door once more.

My fingers wrap around the iron bar that keeps the door closed. I take a deep breath, let it out slowly, and lift the bar. It screeches, metal against metal, but eventually slides free. The door pushes open just a few inches.

I refuse to shut my eyes against the bright light because I need to be prepared in case he is nearby. I wait for several seconds, braced for him to rush me, but nothing happens. Pushing the door open a little wider, I see an expanse of forest. Mostly Coulter pines along with some oak and bay laurel.

I take a tentative step out of the shipping container, my bare feet feeling the pinch of rocks, sticks, and the undergrowth of the forest.

Continuing, I take in my surroundings. At first, I think I'm in the middle of nowhere, hopelessly surrounded by dense forest, which means my chances of getting help are low. But then I peer through some of the trees, spotting a wooden cabin about forty yards away.

Instinctively, I know it's *his* house.

To my horror, the side door opens and my stalker steps out onto a small porch. He's holding a tray with what appears to be some food and a bottle of water on it. His gaze is down as he navigates the three steps, but when his foot hits the ground, he looks up.

His eyes lock with mine. First, they widen in shock and then incredible anger as he realizes his captive has gotten loose.

The man doesn't hesitate. He drops the tray, bolting straight toward me.

Every survival instinct within me kicks in. I turn and run as well. Straight into the deep forest without looking back. I ignore the stabbing jabs of pain in my feet as rocks cut into me, and I don't let branches smacking me in the face slow me down. I grip onto the Taser as hard as I can, and I push my way deeper into the gloom created by a thick canopy above.

I run for what seems like forever, not daring to glance back even once. It will only slow me down. I need to run hard and fast for as long as I can. Try to put distance between us.

My ears strain to hear something that will let me know how close he is, but my own huffing, gasping breaths and the crunch of foliage drowns everything out.

After what feels like miles but was probably only a football field or two in length, I spot a boulder up ahead. I run straight at it. When I reach its edge, I come to a sliding halt. Turning quickly, I brace to meet my attacker head-on in case he is on my heels. I hold the Taser out in front of me, ready to pull the trigger, but I don't see him anywhere. I'm gasping harshly, my lungs completely depleted as I wait for him to rush me.

There's nothing.

But that doesn't mean I'm safe. Turning, I make my way past the boulder. I start running again, trying to put more distance between me and the crazy man who wants to kill me.

CHAPTER 29

Kynan

W HEN MY VEHICLE gets close to Joslyn's signal on the map, I stop on the side of a dirt road a good two hundred yards away. I don't want the sound of my engine alerting anyone of my approach. It takes me only moments to make sure I'm fully locked and loaded. Pistol in a shoulder holster, along with one on my ankle. Hunting knife strapped to my hip in a sheath.

I make a quick call to Cruce and Saint on the connected conference line to let them know I've arrived. The exact address of Joslyn's stalker is no longer a secret, and the police are headed here as well. When I was only a few miles out from Joslyn's signal, Bebe had called us to let us know she had identified the man.

Using a quick program she had coded to run the partial license plate Cruce had gotten, along with the make and model of the vehicle, she cross-referenced that information with the geo-tracking signal from Joslyn's earrings. It came up with an address to a Scott Carlisle.

Age thirty-two, single, and a software developer in

Silicon Valley. He also owned a cabin on the border of the Santa Ynez Mountains, which he purchased about thirty days after Joslyn moved into her new home in Santa Barbara.

He had clearly been planning the abduction for a while. Knowing he had just purchased this property before breaking into her home, I have to deduce he was not attempting to kill her then but only trying to subdue her. That this man had plans for Joslyn sickens me deep in my gut. I don't think I can bear to even try to comprehend.

As it stands, I plan on murdering him quickly rather than slowly. I don't want anything to change that.

Cruce and Saint are less than seven miles away, but I'm not going to wait. Even if this fucker has no intention of killing Joslyn right away, he could be hurting her as we speak.

I grab my phone, the red blinking circle my only focus as I decide to approach from the east rather than coming straight up his driveway. With that in mind, I plunge into the woods and start making my way toward the small, twelve-hundred-foot cabin that sits deep in the woods. Bebe had sent me Google satellite photos of the place. She was also able to hack into his credit cards, revealing he'd purchased a large metal shipping container that was delivered just two days before he broke into her house.

I know exactly what I'm looking for, but I don't know what I'm going to find once I get there.

I pick my way through the pines and scrub laurel, checking the map every five yards or so to make sure I'm on course to sneak in undetected. About fifty yards into the woods, I'm stunned when I see the red light start to move. I watch it for a few seconds before I bolt into action. It's moving away from me at a fast pace. In my heart of hearts, I know Joslyn is running for her life.

I no longer worry about a sneak approach. Instead, I take off running through the dense forest, periodically glancing between the terrain and the map to keep my bearings. I'm probably less than two hundred yards from her—not being able to see her but relying solely on the phone in my hand—when I hear her scream. It sends a burst of adrenaline so deeply through me that my feet turn into rockets, and I fly. Trees and branches whipping past me, I frantically search for anything that will tell me what is going on.

And then I burst out of thick copse and see them.

Joslyn is on her back in the underbrush of fallen pine needles and twigs. Her attacker is on top of her with his hands locked around her throat. She's writhing and bucking and scratching at him.

Like a charging bull, I take off and head directly at them. He hears me coming at the last moment, turning his face sideways—eyes widening in shock as I bolt at him like a thundering locomotive. I lower my shoulder and plow into the man, lifting him clear off Joslyn's body. We both go crashing to the forest floor.

We hit hard, but I take the brunt of it as the force of my impact had me hitting the ground first with him on top of me. With a hard grunt, I roll immediately to my feet and reach for my gun. I have it pulled, cocked, and aimed at his head before he even struggles to his feet.

I spare the briefest of glances at Joslyn to see her scrambling to her feet. Her appearance tells me I'm not sure I'm going to be able to kill him quickly.

She's got red marks around her throat, and the left side of her face is red and swollen. There are dark purple marks all over her body, along with cuts and bloody welts that are probably from her panicked flight into the forest. She takes a few halting steps toward me and falters, falling to her knees. When I look down at her feet, I realize they're covered in blood.

My gaze goes back to Scott Carlisle, and I promise him retribution. "Going to fucking kill you."

Scott grins, his teeth flashing as he starts to laugh. "No, you're not. You're the good guys. You have a moral obligation to turn me over to the police."

With the gun pointed at his head, I take three paces and come to a stop with the barrel planted right between his eyes. To give him credit, he doesn't flinch.

Much.

I push the gun harder into his head, and he rocks backward. "Don't even think you know anything about me," I growl.

Scott sneers. "I know your girl feels mighty fine. Had a good old time with her before you showed up."

"That's a lie," Joslyn screams, and I cut my eyes to her. She's adamantly shaking her head. "He didn't touch me that way, Kynan. Don't do something you're going to regret."

Scott starts laughing, and it sounds maniacal. He throws his thumb over his shoulder at Joslyn, who is still sitting on the ground behind him. "Isn't that sweet? She's trying to protect me."

"So he doesn't kill you, you fucking creep," Joslyn shrieks. "I don't want that on his conscience."

I push the barrel of my gun into Carlisle's forehead and tilt my head, giving him a sly smile.

"Don't worry honey," I say to Joslyn, my eyes pinned on the man. "Where this guy is concerned, I don't have a conscience. It would be nothing for me to pull this trigger and splatter his brains all over the pine trees."

"You seem like a pretty bad-ass guy," Scott muses. "But I have to wonder how much of that bravery is because you have a gun and I don't?"

Before I can answer, I hear rustling in the trees. Without taking my eyes off Scott Carlisle, I listen attentively to the sounds. I know who it is, and I'm not surprised when Cruce and Saint come bursting through the foliage. Saint looks utterly ridiculous in his expensive silk suit.

"You guys caught up to me a lot faster than I thought you would," I drawl. I nod toward Joslyn. "Saint… be a gentleman and give your jacket to my girl."

"She's not your girl," Scott snaps, sounding like a petulant child. "I've marked her. She'll never fully belong to you."

"He's lying," Joslyn screams again, and I spend a brief second of my attention to see Saint covering her with his big coat. He kneels beside her, then takes one of her hands to examine the wounds around her wrist, which are caked with dried blood.

Scott sneers when I glare. He's still under the delusion he is going to be turned over to the police.

Making a decision, I lower my gun. I put a hand to the middle of Scott's chest, then shove him roughly backward. He can't hold his balance, wind-milling his arms in vain before falling to the ground. I holster my gun. "Get up. You've got one chance to come out of this alive. I'm going to fight you fairly."

Scott tosses his head back, hands planted onto the forest floor. "I can't take you in a fight, Kynan. You're former British Special Forces. You clearly work out. Sadly, I don't. I put all of my energy into exercising my brain, which makes me infinitely smarter than you.

Smart enough to know I can't ever hope to win in a fight, so if you don't mind... I'm just going to wait for the police to come."

I reach to my side and grab my hunting knife, slowly pulling it out of the sheath. It's eight inches of lethal steel. "I'm not calling the police. And I said this would be a fair fight."

He watches with wide eyes as I flip the knife into the air, catching it by the blade before immediately slinging it at him. It buries into the forest floor right between his legs. "Pick it up. You have a weapon. I don't. Now let's go."

Scott slowly rises, tugging hard at the knife to dislodge it from the ground. While he does that, I remove my shoulder and knife holsters, tossing them toward Cruce so they are safely out of the way. He bends and picks them up, taking several paces backward to give us some space. It's a silent acknowledgment he is standing down, letting me finish this the way I want to.

Saint is clearly concerned about what I'm going to do. I don't know this man, but when he finally nods his approval to me, I know he's got my back as well.

Turning to face Carlisle, I hold my arms wide, motioning with my fingers for him to come at me.

He glances from me to the knife in his hand and then back to me. Pivoting slightly, he scans Cruce and then Saint, perhaps wondering if they're going to step in and stop this. They both just stare daggers back, making their allegiance clear.

Joslyn merely stares blank faced, and I have no clue what she wants me to do.

Not that it matters. This is going to be finished to *my* satisfaction. He hurt the woman I love, and now he has to pay the ultimate price. Prison is too good for him.

Carlisle finally turns his attention to the knife before raising his gaze to me. He tilts his head, giving me a small smile. "Let's do this."

He comes charging at me, screaming like a banshee. I keep my body loose, rolling on the balls of my feet as he approaches. The knife is raised high, and I keep my eyes pinned on it. He makes a slashing motion at my chest as he reaches me, and I nimbly step to the side. As he barrels past, I give him a backhanded fist to the neck. He goes flying into a tree, then hits it so hard the knife is dislodged from his hand before he crumples to the ground.

"Please tell me that's not all you got," I mutter as I advance on him.

Grabbing him by the back of his blue sweatshirt, I haul him to his feet. He's rattled, but completely conscious and alert. I shove him toward where the knife fell, and he falls to his knees.

"Pick it up," I order.

Carlisle crawls to the knife, grabs it, then struggles to

his feet. He's completely winded, but he also knows he has to fight me.

Once again, he lunges, swinging wildly. I easily grab the wrist holding the knife, then drive my elbow into his forearm, feeling immense satisfaction when the bones audibly crack. Carlisle screams in pain, the knife tumbling from his hand.

Once again, I shove him to the ground. Curling up, he starts moaning. "You broke my fucking arm."

Ignoring him, I walk over to the knife. I pick it up, flip it so the blade is in my hand, and twist toward him. Striding casually to the motherfucker, I hand the knife to him. He reluctantly takes it in his nondominant hand, staring at it.

"Get up."

He shakes his head.

"Get up," I snarl.

He tosses the knife aside. Shaking his head again, he cradles his broken arm. "I'm done. Call the police. Take me into custody. I am not fighting you."

Unacceptable. I reach down and haul him to his feet. Cocking my arm, I let my fist fly right into his face. Dead center on his nose. More bones crunch.

Scott goes flying backward, blood spraying from his nostrils. On his back on the ground, he tries to start crab walking away from me.

I advance on him, intent on beating him to death

since he won't engage with me. Takes a little of the fun out of it, but I can work with what I'm given.

He scuttles away from me, using only his feet and his one good arm until he hits the trunk of a large pine tree. I bend toward him, intent on pulling him up so I can beat him back down, but I'm halted by a soft hand on my shoulder.

"Don't," Joslyn says in a mere whisper, but it has the force of a bomb to my ears. I turn slightly to regard her.

My sweet beautiful Joslyn. The love of my life who is battered, bruised, and bloodied by this psychopath. And she has just asked me not to hurt him anymore.

She steps into me, puts her palms on my face, and says, "Please don't. I know you don't care if it's on your conscience, but it will be on mine if I can't stop you from doing this."

Christ. Every bit of rage, along with the need for vengeance, slithers right out of me, leaving a black greasy trail in its wake. Because it would hurt her if I did this, I have no choice but to stand down. I don't even bother to argue with her, because her words are enough. Her asking me to do something is enough.

"Okay, kitten."

She smiles and goes to her tiptoes, pressing her lips softly to mine. When she pulls back, her face is filled with gratitude and relief. "Thank you for coming to get me."

I vaguely realize Cruce and Saint have yanked Carlisle to his feet and are marching him toward his cabin.

I let my eyes roam over Joslyn's face, wondering how long it's going to take her to heal from these events physically and emotionally.

"I'm so sorry he got you, honey," I say apologetically. "I should have never let you leave my side."

She shakes her head adamantly. "Don't you dare. This was all my fault for falling for his lies. And for the record, I'm not going to let you leave my side again."

I can't help but smile. "Is that a promise?"

Her return smile is tart, and I see the strength in her gaze. "It's a fact. Get used to it."

CHAPTER 30

Joslyn

IT'S HARD TO believe that less than nine hours ago, I had been locked up in a shipping container after having been kidnapped by a psychopath. Now I'm back in the safety of my own home, surrounded by old friends and new... as well as the man I love.

I'm exhausted, but I don't want to show it. I can't because everyone wanted to come over to see me.

To celebrate my safety.

To perhaps see with their own eyes I am indeed okay.

Kynan wanted to chase everyone away. I assured him I was completely fine. Told him I wanted to pop some champagne to celebrate our victory.

It's been a rough day for sure. After Kynan rescued me, I grudgingly agreed to allow an ambulance to transport me to the hospital. Kynan rode along with me, which is the only reason I agreed to it. Scott Carlisle was handcuffed, then led off by the sheriff's department. Lynn later reported he was booked on charges of kidnapping, assault, battery, and attempted murder. I'm fairly sure he'll never step outside of prison again.

I've spent some time wondering if I did the right thing by stopping Kynan. There's no doubt in my mind he would have beaten the man to death, which would have ensured my absolute safety in the future. Ultimately, I just couldn't let him go through with it. Deep down inside, I realized those actions are not the man I know and love. He was being driven by rage because of what Carlisle had done to me and wanted to do to me. Kynan hadn't been seeing reason. Not to mention there'd been a damn good chance Kynan could've gone to prison if he'd killed the man, even though I'm sure all witnesses involved—that would be Saint, Cruce, and me—would have sworn he was only defending his own life in a classic case of self-defense.

The hospital was the worst—not because it hurt like hell getting my injuries treated, particularly my feet—but because there were injuries I hadn't been sure about. It was awful because I'd been asked by the doctor if I needed a rape kit, and I honestly hadn't known the answer. I was ninety-five percent sure he hadn't touched me in that way because I couldn't feel anything. Surely if a woman had been raped, she should be able to know, right? But I had been drugged, so I ultimately told the doctor I should probably have an examination. Kynan ended up breaking down at that point, and it killed me to watch as he put his hands on his face and wept.

It hadn't made it any better when the doctor later confirmed I had not been violated. It was traumatic enough in both my mind and Kynan's to know it had been a possibility.

I was at the hospital for a few hours, and everyone congregated there to wait for me. Detective Kitchner came to interview Kynan, Saint, Cruce, and me. My mom and Darren were obviously there, although they stayed in the waiting room while I'd been treated. I'm sure my mother would have wanted to be in there with me, but in this instance, I think she stepped aside for Kynan to claim his role as my main and primary protector.

Jerico, Bebe, and Rachel had caught a private jet out of Vegas, then drove straight to the hospital where they joined everyone else in the waiting room. Lynn and Harry as well. When I was finally discharged and brought out in a wheelchair, my feet heavily bandaged, it had been incredibly overwhelming to see them all smiling in relief and love. My mom cried, so, of course, I did, too. I'd known everyone except Jerico, but that hadn't stopped him from giving me a massive hug once Kynan introduced us. Knowing he, Bebe, and Rachel had come just to support Kynan—and hopefully see me alive and well—prompted me to invite everyone to the house.

Kynan had *not* been happy about it. Had even tried

to countermand my offer.

We had our first real fight right there in the emergency room lobby, me in a wheelchair and Kynan bending over me, arguing until he was red in the face.

I won though, and Cruce stopped by the store on the way to pick up champagne while Harry went to In-N-Out Burger and got a buttload of food.

Of course, Kynan carried me into my house and settled me in a big chair with pillows under my feet on the ottoman. From my throne, I entertained my guests. My mother hovered unnecessarily, but I didn't mind. Ultimately, Darren chased her away to give others a chance to sit on the couch and talk to me. To have a few moments whereby they could ensure I was indeed okay on all counts.

Cruce and Saint doled out glasses of champagne, and Harry passed out burgers and fries. It was the best party I've ever been to in my entire life.

"Sure you don't want a little champagne?" Lynn asks from the couch, interrupting my internal musings. Lynn had rushed in once my mother vacated her seat.

"I'm good." I'd had half a glass a little earlier. If I had more, I'd probably be passed out given all I'd been through today.

Lynn wrinkles her nose at my denial of such a good bubbly, but moves to refill her own glass from an opened bottle of champagne on the coffee table. Because she is tipsy, she over pours, and it froths all over her. We both laugh. Rachel, who sees the mishap, comes running with some paper towels to clean her up.

I glance into the kitchen where the men are congregated. Jerico, Kynan, Saint, and Cruce. They make a damn fine-looking team, and I'm not just talking about their abilities. They are just damn good-looking men.

Kynan's gaze drifts over to me, which he's done about every two minutes or so since we came home, I suppose just to check to make sure I'm alive and breathing. When he smiles, I return it before giving my attention back to Lynn. She raises her champagne glass, not to toast me but to point an accusing finger.

"I cannot believe you got in that man's car because you thought he had me," she mutters.

"I didn't know it was a fake photo." My exasperation comes out clearly.

"I'm not talking about that," she says with a dismissive wave. "I'm talking about risking your life for mine. You shouldn't have done that."

"Do you how hard it is to find a good manager? I mean, come on, Lynn, I was not about to let you go."

She snorts and rolls her eyes before taking another healthy glug of champagne. I expect she's going to be sleeping in one of the guest rooms tonight.

Bebe comes walking into the living room, carrying a bottle of water. She's the only one who did not partake of the alcohol, and I wonder why.

I don't know her well enough to ask, so I let it go.

She takes a seat on the opposite end of the couch from Lynn, then settles into it. Shooting me a wry smile, she says, "I honestly think prison may have been preferable to the stress you put me under today, Joslyn. I think I'd like to go back."

I burst out laughing, and she chuckles along with me.

Shaking her head, she says, "Seriously… This whole experience shaved a couple of years off my life."

"If I didn't have gashes in my feet, I'd get up right now to hug you." My words are sincere. "Thanks to you, I'm alive."

Bebe waves her hand, shaking her head again. "It was a definite team effort."

Tilting my head, I study this woman who's been pretty much locked away for the past seven years without any real human contact because she was in solitary. She is so kind, loyal, and empathetic. She's gone above and beyond to work to save a woman she doesn't even know. And I have to think there are remarkable things coming down the line for a woman such as this.

"Thank you, Bebe." There's no mistaking the gratefulness in my voice. "You are a true treasure to Kynan and Jameson Force Security. I can never repay you for what you did for me."

"Oh, don't worry about that," Kynan says as he

walks up to my chair. He bends, scoops me up in his arms, then positions himself to sit in my place, settling me squarely on his lap. He nods at Bebe. "She's getting a huge bonus."

Bebe holds up her water bottle in salute. "I am not going to say no to that."

I swear the cue could not have been any more perfect, because at that moment, my doorbell rings. I can't help but smile at what I know is on the other side. It's better than any bonus Bebe could get.

Today is the day her mom and son are coming to visit. Of course, Kynan did not account for the fact she would hop on a jet plane with Jerico and Rachel and screw up his glorious plans for an emotional, heartfelt reunion. When he saw Bebe in the emergency room lobby, he immediately got busy changing plans.

Kynan worked his magic, managing to get Bebe's family on the next private plane out of Las Vegas to Santa Barbara.

Cruce must be in on what is going on because he immediately goes to the front door, just out of sight from where I'm sitting. Bebe doesn't even know anything is going on. She and Lynn are casually chatting. I see Cruce walking into the great room. He comes up behind Bebe, followed by a woman who looks exactly like her daughter. Raven-black hair worn in a shoulder-length bob with the same high cheekbones and delicate nose as

Bebe. And right behind her is a miniature duplicate of Bebe herself. Her son has the same bluish-black hair and crystal blue eyes as his mother.

My own eyes immediately fill up with tears, knowing what an emotional reunion this is going to be. Unfortunately, Bebe happens to glance at me as I start crying and becomes alarmed.

"Are you okay, Joslyn?" she asks, starting to rise from the couch.

Kynan just chuckles, and Bebe glares at him for his supposed insensitivity.

I can't help myself, so I nod toward her mom and son who are standing just behind the couch. "You have someone here to see you."

Bebe turns around slowly. The minute her eyes land on her mom and son, she falls to her knees and starts sobbing. Of course, I lose my shit and do the same. Lynn also starts crying. Kynan just groans, hugging me tightly.

Bebe doesn't stay down, though. Her excitement has her immediately popping up with tears streaming down her face. She rushes around the couch where she scoops her son into her arms. Holding him tight, she buries her face in his neck. Her mother approaches, then works her way into the family embrace. They hug each other for the longest time while plenty of tears are shed. I turn sideways to cuddle against Kynan, and he squeezes me sweetly.

Eventually, Bebe is able to regain her composure to make introductions all the way around. She brings her mother and son up to my chair, and I feel stupid for not being able to get up. Kynan, though, seems completely comfortable with the way things are. We both shake Bebe's mom's hand, and Gloria Grimshaw profusely thanks Kynan for arranging this trip. Then Bebe puts her hands on her son's shoulders. At just nine years old, it's obvious Aaron Grimshaw is going to be a good-looking man when he grows up. Right now, though, he is incredibly shy as his mom makes the introductions. But adorably, he musters up enough courage to look Kynan in the eye and say, "Thank you for getting my mom out of prison."

There is no hiding the emotion in Kynan's voice when he tells Aaron gruffly, "No problem, kid."

Bebe moves off to make further introductions. Lynn vacates the couch, then totters into the kitchen. It leaves Kynan and me alone in the great room, snuggled in the big overstuffed chair with his long legs crossed on the ottoman. I burrow in deeper to his side and whisper, "I have a confession to make."

He pulls his chin inward. "What's that?"

"I think I might be getting a little tired," I admit sheepishly. "But I don't want everyone to leave. They're all having so much fun."

Expecting Kynan to come up with a graceful exit

plan, I'm completely stunned when he just pushes off the chair with me in his arms, cradling me like a baby. He turns to the crowd, now all in the kitchen talking and laughing. "Everyone… Joslyn is tired and we're going to bed. Don't break anything."

Everyone shouts out good nights and farewells, and I'm completely mortified he would just leave them all to their own devices while I am the hostess. Kynan starts walking me to my bedroom, so I call over his shoulder to my guests, "Help yourself to anything. You should all take a guest room. There are extra blankets and pillows in the linen closet. Have fun."

In my bedroom, Kynan could not be more caring or gentle in his ministrations. While I would really kill for a shower or bath, I'm frankly too tired and there's no easy way to do it without having to remove all of my bandages. I settle for him removing my clothes and helping me into one of his T-shirts. He strips down to his boxer briefs, then settles into the bed beside me. While I'm tired and exhausted, I'm also slightly exhilarated to be alive.

I'm deliriously happy to be cuddled next to this man who not only literally saved my life, but also rejuvenated my entire soul merely by coming back into my world.

Kynan sits up against the headboard, and I move closer into his side. He puts a big arm around me and holds me gently, twisting to plant a tender kiss on my forehead.

"Big day, huh?" he asks.

I snort in response. "The biggest.

Kynan shrugs. "I don't know. I bet we could outdo it."

"How could we possibly outdo today?"

Another shrug from him. "Disneyland? Paris? Rome? Those are just a few ideas off the top of my head."

I giggle in response. "I love Disneyland. Let's go. Once I'm back up on my feet, anyway. I mean that both metaphorically and physically."

Kynan chuckles. We fall silent, the gravity of the day starting to push down upon us.

After several moments, Kynan's voice comes across the quiet. "When I got your text, Jos... I literally thought my life was over. When I realized he had you— it was the darkest moment I've ever had in my entire existence."

I push up so I can look at him. "I'm sorry. I was so stupid."

He shakes his head, placing his finger on my lips. "No apologies. No recriminations. I only told you so you'd know how much I love you. You are the only reason for my existence, Joslyn. If you are not in my life, I don't exist. It's that simple."

The tears well up in my eyes because that is without a doubt the most loving, genuine, and reaffirming thing

I've ever heard. The fact it came from Kynan's lips makes it all the more special. "I love you so much, Kynan. You know you're the one who helped me escape."

He cocks an eyebrow. "How's that?"

"I had a dream while I was tied to that chair. I must've fallen asleep because of the drugs he'd given me. And in that dream, you and I were married and had children. We lived in a beautiful, rustic cabin on the outskirts of Pittsburgh. You came home from work, and I was so excited to see you. I just knew my life was complete. I asked you to do something for me. Something ridiculous. Changing an air filter I couldn't reach. And you know what you told me?"

Kynan doesn't say anything but shakes his head, completely drawn in by my story.

"You told me I could do it myself. That I didn't need you to figure it out. When I woke up, I realized even though I knew you were coming for me, I had the power and the ability to do something to help myself in the meantime. So that's when I started working on the ropes, struggling to get free. You gave me that power and confidence. Without you coming back into my life, that just wouldn't have happened."

Kynan dips his head to press his mouth against mine. When he pulls back, he says, "We've been given another shot, kitten. And I certainly don't know what your plans are, but I totally intend to take it."

"I think I'm ready to take it, too." Smiling, I give him what I hope is everything he desires. "You're my life now, Kynan, and I was thinking I could use a break from the West Coast. If you'll have me, I would like to get this party rolling. I'd like to go back to Pittsburgh with you."

A wide smile breaks out on Kynan's face, and he grins from ear to ear. "Are you serious?"

I nod. "I've never been more serious in my life."

"Then you have made me the happiest man in the world."

EPILOGUE

One month later...

KYNAN COMES BARRELING into our apartment, and it scares me so bad I shriek. Putting my hand over my heart, I glare as I pop up from the couch. "You about gave me a damn heart attack."

He grins, not sorry in the least, and strides right up to me. I get a quick, hard kiss on my mouth before he starts pulling me back to the door. "Come on. I have something to show you."

We exit our apartment and he closes the door, not even bothering to lock it. There's no need. The building at Jameson Force Security is as secure as a building can get. The other two residents, Cruce and Saint, would never steal from us. Their apartments are on the same hall but on the opposite side.

Kynan takes the staircase that runs down the center of the entire building. It's my favorite feature about this old warehouse that's been converted into a super-secret, subversive organization that does all kinds of sly things with the government's approval, but would never be acknowledged as such.

I have to run to keep up with him. I'm afraid I'm going to break my neck. "Slow down, Kynan."

He merely growls in that super-hot, alpha way, then scoops me up in his arms. He bounds down the staircase, all the way into the basement where the parking garage is. He's extremely secretive as he loads me up in his Chevy Suburban and we exit out into the seedy part of Pittsburgh.

"Where are we going?" I ask. "New restaurant? You taking me shopping?"

"You'll see," is all he will tell me before he starts whistling.

"Saint and Cruce seem to be settling in nice nicely," I say as a means to start conversation. I know if I can get Kynan talking, he might slip up and give me a hint as to where we're going.

Knowing my plan, he's incredibly vague when he merely says, "Yup."

"I had lunch with Bebe and Aaron today," I offer, smiling at how happy Bebe is now to be reunited with her family. They all live together in a small house just on the outskirts of the city. "Aaron is enjoying his new school."

"That's nice," Kynan says with a grin, then turns the radio up.

I sigh with exasperation. "What the hell is going on?"

"How about you just sit back, relax, and enjoy a nice

drive?"

Huffing with frustration, I throw myself back into the seat and cross my arms over my chest, vowing he's not getting sex tonight since he's being so insufferable.

Who am I kidding? I'm totally going to give it up to him because it's just that damn good.

Leaving my life behind in California was the best decision I have ever made. Lynn and Harry were obviously sad to see me go. And while I am not actively working, they are still on my payroll. I never know when something good might come along, and I'm willing to consider everything. But for right now, I'm enjoying spending my time with Kynan. While he's working, I spend my time writing music that feeds my soul. I have no clue if I will ever do anything with it, but it is making me happy right now.

Being with Kynan and starting a new life with him has become an absolute dream come true. There is no doubt he is my soul mate, and I believe the monstrous asshole called fate put Scott Carlisle in my life so Kynan and I could be reunited. I believe deeply within my soul that, in some weird way, I have a bit of gratitude toward that psychopath.

Scott Carlisle was arraigned in the Santa Barbara County court two days after he was arrested, and bail was denied. He'll be in jail until his trial, and the district attorney promised me an easy conviction.

We head out of the city moving north, but I don't know my way around yet. Within fifteen minutes, I'm totally lost. We're amidst rolling hills, with the bright lights of the city far behind us.

Kynan reaches over and takes my hand in his, pulling it across the console to his mouth where he kisses the back of it.

He simultaneously turns on the right signal, and we enter a gravel road.

I have the weirdest sense of what feels like déjà vu, but it's not. I've never been here, but it feels familiar.

When we come around the curve, a mountain cabin appears. It doesn't look exactly like the one in my dreams, but I told Kynan enough about it that he came damn close. There's a *for sale* sign by the mailbox.

I look at him, but he keeps his eyes on the driveway until he brings the Suburban to a stop. He finally gives me his attention. With a smile, he gestures through the windshield at the cabin. "What do you think?"

I slowly turn, scanning the house. It's not overly grand in scale, but it's certainly big enough to house us with room for expansion. "It's beautiful."

"I'm sure glad you think so because I already bought it," he says, and I snap my head in his direction.

"You already bought it?"

"For us," he clarifies.

"But we're fine in the apartment," I say sincerely. "I

don't need all this."

"Do you need this?" he asks slyly, then he's holding out a black jewelry box so it's hovering in front of my face.

I blink at it stupidly as he pops it open. Inside is a beautiful diamond engagement ring. I'm absolutely dazzled not by the jewelry, but by the significance of this moment.

My eyes search his, heart thundering when he asks, "Will you marry me, Joslyn? Make my life complete? Be my wife and give me babies? I'll even buy you a dog."

I'd always wondered if I'd be speechless or have a ready answer when this moment came.

That is not a curiosity any longer. I throw myself at him, wrapping my arms tightly around his neck. "The answer is yes. Yes. Yes. Yes."

Kynan squeezes me hard, pressing into my neck. We stay like that a long moment, but then he's pushing me away and pulling the ring out of the box.

It's stunning. A round-cut diamond, several carats in size, surrounded by smaller diamonds on the outside as well as along the band. It's classic and elegant, and I couldn't have picked anything more perfect.

Kynan's hands are trembling as he slides the ring on my finger, then he pulls it up to his mouth so he can kiss it.

He regards me with so much love on his face I'm

humbled. "You're the best thing that has ever happened to me. I know we can't get that twelve years back. But, frankly, I don't want them. You and I became who we are because we were apart, and I love you even more today than I did back then. I cannot wait to move forward through the rest of this life with you by my side, Joslyn."

Of course, tears come to my eyes. I start to sniffle. I've never been as elegant in spontaneous conversation as this suave Brit, but I speak from my heart.

"My soul is so full right now, Kynan. It actually kind of hurts because it's so full of you. And yet, I don't want to feel any other way. I cannot wait to marry you—to get pregnant and raise children together."

Kynan smiles before tipping his head to place his lips upon mine. It's the sweetest, most promising kiss I've ever felt in my life. I have to wonder how I got to be as lucky as I am, but I'll have the rest of my life with Kynan to figure it out.

The suspense continues at Jameson Force Security with *Code Name: Sentinel (Jameson Force Security, Book #2)*, coming September 10, 2019!
GO HERE to pre-order Code Name: Sentinel now.
sawyerbennett.com/bookstore/code-name-sentinel

Go here to see other works by Sawyer Bennett:
https://sawyerbennett.com/bookshop

Don't miss another new release by Sawyer Bennett!!! Sign up for her newsletter and keep up to date on new releases, giveaways, book reviews and so much more.
https://sawyerbennett.com/signup

Connect with Sawyer online:

Website: sawyerbennett.com
Twitter: twitter.com/bennettbooks
Facebook: facebook.com/bennettbooks
Instagram: instagram.com/sawyerbennett123
Book+Main Bites:
bookandmainbites.com/sawyerbennett
Goodreads: goodreads.com/Sawyer_Bennett
Amazon: amazon.com/author/sawyerbennett
BookBub: bookbub.com/authors/sawyer-bennett

About the Author

Since the release of her debut contemporary romance novel, Off Sides, in January 2013, Sawyer Bennett has released multiple books, many of which have appeared on the New York Times, USA Today and Wall Street Journal bestseller lists.

A reformed trial lawyer from North Carolina, Sawyer uses real life experience to create relatable, sexy stories that appeal to a wide array of readers. From new adult to erotic contemporary romance, Sawyer writes something for just about everyone.

Sawyer likes her Bloody Marys strong, her martinis dirty, and her heroes a combination of the two. When not bringing fictional romance to life, Sawyer is a chauffeur, stylist, chef, maid, and personal assistant to a very active daughter, as well as full-time servant to her adorably naughty dogs. She believes in the good of others, and that a bad day can be cured with a great work-out, cake, or even better, both.

Sawyer also writes general and women's fiction under the pen name S. Bennett and sweet romance under the name Juliette Poe.